W9-CSG-725

Schizo

Schizo

Kim Firmston

James Lorimer & Company Ltd., Publishers
Toronto

James Lorimer & Company Ltd., Publishers acknowledges the support of the Ontario Arts Council. We acknowledge the financial support of the Government of Canada through the Canada Book Fund for our publishing activities. We acknowledge the support of the Canada Council for the Arts which last year invested $20.1 million in writing and publishing throughout Canada. We acknowledge the Government of Ontario through the Ontario Media Development Corporation's Ontario Book Initiative.

Cover Image: iStockphoto

Library and Archives Canada Cataloguing in Publication

Firmston, Kim
    Schizo / Kim Firmston.

(SideStreets)
Issued also in an electronic format.
ISBN 978-1-55277-872-2 (bound).--ISBN 978-1-55277-871-5 (pbk.)

    1. Schizophrenia--Juvenile fiction. I. Title. II. Series: SideStreets

PS8611.I75S35 2011   jC813'.6 C2011-903128-0

James Lorimer &   Distributed in the United
Company Ltd., Publishers   States by:
317 Adelaide Street West,   Orca Book Publishers
Suite #1002   P.O. Box 468
Toronto, ON, Canada   Custer, WA USA
M5V 1P9   98240-0468
www.lorimer.ca

Printed and bound in Canada.
Manufactured by Webcom in Toronto, Ontario, Canada in August, 2011.
Job #379091

Chapter 1

There's a crash and bang. A drawer slams shut.

"Damn it!"

Her voice breaks through the apartment door.

"Pencils!"

She was asleep when I left.

"It's three seven. Three seven. Three seven."

The chanting crawls into my brain. Settles in my skull. I shiver. Another crash echoes through the door, making my heart pick up speed. Paper rustles. Large sheets torn from an oversized pad, the kind they use for school lectures. My mother is on one of her rampages. Briefly, I consider running, but I then I think of Dustin — and can't. Crap. I hate coming home with her like this.

"Three seven!" Mom shouts again.

I slide my key into the lock and twist.

"Why can't it be four six? Everything should be four six."

Slowly I push open the apartment door, my fingers white on the doorknob. I tiptoe through the darkened living room, careful not to brush against the employee-of-the-month awards that barely hang on the wall or knock over the clock with the three, five, and seven scratched out.

My mother is bent over the dining room table, dirty-blond hair spastic, her pencil working furiously. Huge sheets of paper surround her, numbers on some of them, diagrams on others. She's directly between me and the hall that leads to our bedrooms. I'm going to get a lecture.

"Daniel! Were you hiding?" She starts laughing. It's eerie. "Come here. You have to see how the numbers have changed!"

I approach, hands out, trying to shush her. It's after two in the morning. My ear strains to hear any movement from Dustin's room. Nothing so far.

"Look!" Mom points at the long series of numbers running down the nearest paper. They fall in a lopsided rainbow. It looks like how my writing ends up when I don't use lined paper, all slanting to the lower right. She's drawn buildings too. The science centre maybe, the Calgary Tower, the Bay downtown — all rough but recognizable. More numbers loop and cascade over the buildings before they are contained in complicated swirling shapes. Some numbers are written again and again, one on top of the other, darkening the paper until there are holes.

"Look Daniel. The sevens are trying to take over. The sevens are tipping the balance." She leans close, whispers in my ear, her breath hot and damp. "It's up to us," she says. "We have to keep the nice numbers, the safe numbers, together. Sixes and fours." She grabs another paper with a large half-finished sketch of my school, Western Canada High. "See here? Threes and sevens. It's riddled with them. It's not safe. Not anymore. You have to stay away. Never go there again." My mom's eyes dance, unfocused. Her elegant face is pinched. She grabs my arm, her polished nails biting through my jacket. "It's for your own safety. Stay home. Stay home!" She's shrieking by the end.

"Calm down," I plead. I'm sure she's going to wake Dustin.

She grabs my shoulders and yanks me hard. The taste of coffee left over from the Night Owl Café turns sour on my tongue.

"No school," she says a little more quietly.

"But I have a test tomorrow," I explain.

"This," she shouts, her hands clawing the paper, "this is a test! We have to stay together! You have to stay safe!"

Our neighbour, Mr. Jones, bangs from the other side of the wall. "Shut up, crazy woman!" he yells.

I grab the sheet of paper from her hand and smooth it on the table. I trace the soft, pencil-smudged numbers with my finger. Strange addition and subtraction that wouldn't make sense even to the most brilliant mathematician. "Oh, yeah. I see. Here, right?" I pretend to understand. "Okay. No school for me. But Dustin is safe, isn't he?"

She nods, her laugh cracking the air between us. "I chose his school for a reason. It's so, so safe there." She grabs the paper back and grips her pencil with white-fingered tightness. "*They* chose your school. I had nothing to do with it. And even when I showed the School Council how to make it safe, by changing the name and firing the principal, *they* wouldn't do it. They just stared at me. I don't even think they understood the budget I made." Mom brushes her hand in front of her face, her eyes following something that's not there. "That blond one looked especially blank. Telling me the School Council's job was communication and providing better materials to help students learn." Mom turns her attention back to the paper and makes a quick note before looking up at me. "Wouldn't a budget do that?"

I nod. "Sure."

"Now they want something. All of them. The numbers prove it."

"What?" I ask, momentarily getting caught up in my mother's madness.

She grabs a blank paper and starts scribbling. "I'm not sure. I have to sort it out."

"It's late." I say, laying my hand over her writing. "You must be tired. Why don't you do these calculations in the morning?"

She straightens and frowns. "The numbers are

talking to me right now, Daniel. You know I hear them better at night. I'll go to bed when they're done."

"Did you take your pill yet?" I ask, going to the kitchen and taking down the pink cardboard box. The blister pack inside shows that there are only two pills left. "You're almost out. You should go to the drop-in clinic tomorrow and get some more." I punch out the second-last pill and run a glass of water, heading back to my mom and handing them to her.

She makes a face. "These things make me fat," she says.

"You look great." I smile.

"They make me dizzy and confused. The numbers don't do that. I don't see how these pills are better."

"Please, Mom," I beg.

She pops the pill into her mouth and takes a gulp of the water. "There. Happy?" She pulls me down to kiss me on the top of my head. "Now leave me alone. I have work to do. I'll get you if I need you."

"Okay," I say, thinking how smoothly that went for a change. On the way to my bedroom, I pause to listen at Dustin's door. It's quiet. Maybe he's still asleep.

In my room, I flop onto my bed. I don't even bother changing — after all, in less than five hours I'll have to be up again. Minutes after my eyes close I detect shuffling. In the street-light glow coming through my second story window, I see my doorknob slowly turn. The door inches open. My breath catches before I see a tuft of frizzy brown hair. It's Dustin, my nine-year-old brother. His eyes are big. His brown fingers curl tight around his ratty stuffed dog.

"Can I sleep with you?" he pleads in a whisper.

I nod and motion him over, lifting my blankets.

He shuts the door so silently it reminds me of how many times we've both been through this.

"Thanks Dan." Dustin smiles, tucking himself in and stealing my pillow.

"Did she wake you up?" I ask, laying my head on my arm, and letting my other arm fall over my brother's body.

"Yeah."

"Everything's okay now, and you still have school tomorrow, so get some sleep."

He nods. His eyes close. The clock says two thirty-three. I can still make out my mom's chanting. It's quieter now — more stable. I pull my quilt over my shoulders, already dreading how tired I'm going to feel. Tomorrow is going to be fun. Tons and tons of fun.

Chapter 2

The school clock reads nine eleven. Late again. I run down the hallway to Social Studies sweaty, out of breath, and with the wrong textbook clutched under my arm. Somehow I managed to grab math by mistake. At least the early morning nausea from too little sleep has worn off. Glancing over my shoulder, I scan for stray teachers. Mr. Johnston will still let me in if I don't get nabbed for running in the hallway. My body smashes into something, making me turn to look where I'm going. Chain Gupta stands glaring just outside the classroom door. He lifts his arm and pushes me back.

"Hey! Watch it, Nutbar," he says, thrusting his chest out. He smells of curry and too much body spray. Chain is at least half a foot taller and a good three inches wider than me.

"Don't call me that," I say, moving to walk

around him, my hand going for the doorknob.

"Why?" he asks, shoving me back. "Can't take the truth, Nutbar?"

Chain's been my own personal pain in the ass since fourth grade. He loves to tell stories about my mom's visits to his family's corner store, Gupta's Grocery. The tales always get him a ton of laughs and me a reputation. I was hoping that rep would disappear with the end of grade nine. Western Canada High has so many students, I was sure I could blend in. Disappear. But so far, Chain's been really good about sharing the stories with the larger crowd. I would like to say it warms my heart that he thinks about me so much — but it doesn't.

"I'm not a nutbar," I say, trying to dodge past him.

"No, you're a schizo-nutbar." Chain grins, blocking me, arms crossed like a Punjabi bouncer. "Just like your schizo mom."

"Don't call my mom that. She's sick. You wouldn't call someone with cancer names, would you?" I glare at him. "Well, maybe *you* would. Anyway, she's none of your business."

"She is when she comes in my store muttering and moaning." He puts on a high-pitched voice, pursing his lips like some sort of fish in drag. "There's too many sevens in here. The fives are hiding in the corner. Oh me! Oh my! My sons are in danger!" He laughs. "Sound familiar?"

I don't think. I just tackle. Had a thought

actually crossed my mind, the thought would have been something like: *There is no way you can take Chain Gupta in a fight. He's going to kill you. You are a nutbar.* As it is, we slam against the door. Through the small window, I see everyone in the classroom pop their heads up from their tests. A few snickers are held behind hands. Then the Social Studies teacher, Mr. Johnston, blocks the view. He pulls open the door, making both Chain and I fall in. I look up from the ground.

"Chain! Daniel!" Mr. Johnston yells, his face purple. He looks like an enraged beet. "What is going on?"

We scramble to our feet. Chain somehow manages to look innocent. I try for the same thing, but I think it just makes me look disturbed. A finger appears in my face.

"He started it. I was just trying to get to class on time," Chain says. He straightens his button-up shirt, tucking it into his dress pants.

I try straightening my D.O.A. Class War, Eat the Rich t-shirt while hiding the torn knee of my jeans behind my other leg. It doesn't work. Now I look like I'm disturbed and have to go to the bathroom. "He called my mom names," I say.

Mr. Johnston shakes his head and casts a quick glare at the class, sending them back to their tests. I can still see their eyes dart to catch glimpses of the action. Heather, my only real friend in school, gives me a sympathetic smile.

Mr. Johnston is talking again. "Chain, take a

test from my desk and sit down. Daniel … "

"It's Dan," I correct. I hate Daniel.

"It's Nutbar," Chain says under his breath as he walks away, making me take another swing at him.

"Daniel," Mr. Johnston repeats, "you can wait for me out in the hall. I would like a word."

I wink at Heather, trying to pull off a cool exit. She covers a giggle with her hand and looks down at her test.

Chapter 3

Mr. Johnston stares down his bulbous nose at me. "Everyone else seems to make it on time and enter the classroom without a brawl."

I press my back against the row of cold metal lockers. Man, I am so tired. I could sleep right here. Sleep for a thousand years and not even care when the bell rang or if the school closed for the night. If it weren't for Dustin, I just might.

"Should I make an exception for you?" Mr. Johnston continues. "Ignore the fact that you regularly interrupt my class. Are you so unique that you deserve special treatment? Hmm?"

I catch Chain twirling his finger beside his ear and mouthing the word "mom" through the window. I try to flip him the finger without Mr. Johnston seeing. No such luck.

"Daniel!" Mr. Johnston booms.

"It's Dan." I pull myself straight. "Listen, I'm sorry … "

"It is not my responsibility to run your life, Daniel." Mr. Johnston says, not letting me speak. "However, it is my responsibility to keep an orderly class and I expect my students to arrive promptly and act according to school rules. It's only the middle of October and your attendance has more holes in it than the finest Swiss cheese." Mr. Johnston pauses, obviously pleased by his comparison. "You are not taking your education seriously."

I sigh. Everyone has an agenda. Why fight it. "So," I glance at the closed classroom door, "can I write my test?"

"No. I think it would be best if you had a discussion with the principal instead. He's asked to see you anyway."

I turn, silent, and head up the hallway to the main office, my clenching teeth shooting sharp pains into my head. This year was supposed to be different. Different school, different teachers, more students … I was supposed to be able to start again. Get away from being the joke with the strange mother. I guess things never really change. Not for me, anyway.

The secretary ushers me straight into Mr. Garnnet's office. He's a big man. Used to play football before he went into education. My whole body is the same girth as one of his legs. For the second time this morning, I feel puny.

"Pull up a chair. Is everything okay at home, Daniel?" He gets right to the meat of the matter.

"Dan," I correct, sitting in one of the vinyl-covered visitor seats.

"Dan, right. Your attendance has been very spotty. I have to warn you, we can't tolerate this. If there's a problem, we have excellent counsellors. You can talk to them. Talking can often help."

"I just missed the bus this morning," I say, thinking of the real reasons I was late. Things like waiting for Mom to leave for work so I could sneak off to school, and Dustin insisting I walk him all the way to his classroom. I did miss the bus after that, so I'm not really lying. "It won't happen again."

"Missing the bus seems to be the least of your problems. Six absences since the beginning of school. It's only been a month and a half. Can you explain?"

I think of my mom's calculations. "You wouldn't get it."

"Dan, you can tell me."

I clear my throat and fall back to my old excuses from junior high. "My mom was sick. I had to stay home and help her." Not too far from the truth.

"I'm sorry to hear that. Your mom certainly doesn't look like the sickly type. At the School Council meeting she was full of vim and vigour. In fact, she had lots of ideas about the direction of the school."

I groan inwardly. I know she demanded Mr. Garnnet be replaced.

Mr. Garnnet shuffles some papers on his desk. "I've had a look at the numbers she's suggested for the budget. Very inspired."

"Yeah, Mom is good with her numbers."

"I'd really like to discuss them with her. Perhaps you can ask her to call me."

"Uh, sure," I say, knowing I'll do nothing of the sort.

"And Dan?"

"Yeah?"

"Maybe next time your mom gets sick, it might be best if someone else in your family, maybe an older relative, looks after her."

I nod. That might work, if Mom hadn't chased off all our relatives and then moved away without telling them. "It won't happen again," I repeat.

Mr. Garnnet smiles. His thick fingers grab a sheet of paper and thrust it at me. "On another note, it seems you have yet to pay your school fees. Here's a copy of what you have owing. Please be sure to bring a cheque in tomorrow. If it's a problem you can go to student services and get an application for funding."

"It's not a problem. We can pay."

I look at the bill. I know Mom won't pay the school fees. She doesn't even want me to be here. I'm going to have to get sneaky.

"Is there anything else I can —" Mr. Garnnet starts.

"No." I stand up. "I'm good. Can I go?"

The principal eyes me, like he's trying to understand something. "Are you sure everything is okay?"

I take a deep breath. Straighten my t-shirt. Run my fingers through my sweat-damp hair. "I'm fine. I have a test to write."

"Actually, Mr. Johnston asked that you not interrupt his class. Perhaps you can go to the library and study until your next class."

"Okay." I turn toward the door.

"And Dan," he says to my back. "Try to get more sleep."

Sleep? That almost makes me laugh.

Chapter 4

The librarian is busy helping a Goth girl find an article on the Canadian slave trade as I skulk past and settle into my favourite spot, a quiet corner near the back. The table is cool on my forehead. It's been quite the morning. I can't even think anymore. Can't function. So tired.

My mind drifts. It floats out of my body. I feel as if I'm hovering somewhere near the ceiling. Random images begin to flicker through my head. My mom explaining how she "looks after" numbers as a data entry clerk. Dustin staring at the school doors like it's another challenge he's stuck with. Chain Gupta doing an impression of my mom shopping at Gupta's Grocery.

"Dan?" The voice seems to call from far away. "Are you sleeping?"

I look up, wipe the drool off my cheek and rub my arm across the wet spot on the table. "Um."

It's Heather. She's blond, sweet, and perfectly normal. What a bad mix. She should be staying as far away from me as possible.

According to Heather, we kind of met this past summer at the Night Owl Café. I was playing in their jam session. She was in the audience, too shy to come up and talk to me. When she actually introduced herself at the beginning of school, I didn't believe a word she said. I mean, she's way too normal to have ever hung out at the Night Owl.

But now that I know her better, I think she might have been telling the truth. Heather likes to push the boundaries. Last week she signed herself out of math, claiming she had a dentist appointment, just so she could get ready for the Children of Bodom concert she was seeing with some of her friends.

Heather is pretty crazy about music. All kinds of music — punk, dub, and even classical, but her favourite is heavy metal. Ever since she found out I could play a bit of Black Sabbath on my bass guitar, she's been bugging me to have her over so she can hear it for herself. I've had to say no. I never bring anyone home. Mom's schizophrenia is worse in the evenings. Besides, Chain spreading rumours is bad enough without my mom confirming them.

"Do you have a spare too?" Heather asks.

"Um, no," I answer, trying to get my bearings. I feel all confused and fuzzy. "Got kicked out of Social. Late for a test."

Heather laughs with a bit of a snort. "I'm in Social with you, dork. We're almost done the next period. Where are you supposed to be now?"

"English. I'm late?" I ask dumbly.

"Yup," she says, her blue eyes mischievous. "Fifteen minutes until lunch."

I rub my face. "Crap, crap, crap."

"Come on, it's not that bad."

"I'm going to be expelled."

"Well that calls for a celebration!" Heather cheers. "Come on, I'll buy you lunch. Tubby Dog?"

I peek through my fingers. "Share some T-rings?"

"You know it." Her smile is big and reassuring. I don't know why, it's completely unexplainable, but I feel better.

The sun's shining bright and strong as we head down Seventeenth Avenue. The lunch bell hasn't even rung. I guess I've officially skipped another class. I'm so doomed, but with Heather at my side, I don't really care.

"We're starting a band," she says, completely out of the blue.

"'We' who?"

"Me, Sebastian, and Maggie. We were wondering if you wanted to join."

"What kind of music?" I ask.

"Heavy metal."

Heather's blond hair blows in the breeze like an L.A. supermodel's. I still have a hard time getting my head around her love of that genre. "Metal?"

She laughs. "Sure, why not?"

"I thought you just listened to it," I say. "What instrument do you play?"

"I sing, Sebastian's on guitar, and Maggie plays drums. We need a bassist."

"I play punk. It's a little different."

"Not so much," she says.

"Umm, yeah." I say nothing for a second, thinking I should end this conversation. "When?" It pops out of my mouth before I can stop it.

"After school and on weekends. Whenever we can all get together. Interested?"

Yes, I think, totally interested. But Dustin — I can't leave him alone. Not with Mom. Not when they're both awake. And Mom gets way too freaked when Dustin and I disappear for any length of time. I shake my head. "No. Sorry, I'm too busy."

Heather frowns and pushes open the door to Tubby Dog, letting loose the odour of hot french fries and fiery chili. "You have a job?" she asks.

"I guess. Not paid. I have a little brother."

"So bring him along."

We order T-rings and colas, then grab a table, our eyes on a silent episode of the seventies cartoon, *Super Friends*, as it plays on the white brick wall. "I don't know," I finally say.

"I have a little brother." Heather winks. "They can play together. Come on, it'll be fun."

"Let me think about it."

"What's to think about?"

"At least let me find out if I'm suspended first," I say as our order of T-rings is called out. I get up and grab the greasy container filled with a half-dozen spicy onion rings, each as big as a doughnut.

"Tomorrow then," she says, planting a quick kiss on my cheek that lights off a bright glow of fireworks in my brain.

Jamming is beginning to sound really good.

Chapter 5

At the end of the school day, I do my best to smooth things over with my English teacher, Mrs. Dibbs. She's fair and gives me the assignment I slept through in the library. Then she catches me up on the discussion and reminds me that morning tutorials are really the time all this should be done. I don't think I've ever made it to school early enough to get to tutorials. I'll have to try. It's the only way Mr. Johnston will let me take the test I missed. Otherwise, I'm getting a zero.

At this rate I'm starting to think Mom may be right. Not about the school being evil, but about not coming. I mean, if I've basically failed most of my classes in the first month and a half, why even try? She might be right about the evil thing too, especially when it comes to Mr. Johnston. I head out the doors, twenty minutes late, and grab the bus. It must be a theme today — running behind.

Sebastian, a skinny kid with smooth black hair, pushes through the packed bus to get to me. "Dan! You coming to jam tonight?" he asks. "Heather said —"

I shake my head. "Can't."

"Tomorrow?"

"Nope."

"You don't know what you're missing," he says. "It's gonna be sick."

Actually, I do know what I'm missing and I don't want to think about it. "My stop, sorry," I say, getting off two stops before I need to. If I didn't, I might say something stupid like, "Yeah, I'll come jam with you guys. No problem."

Except everything is a problem when you have a mother like mine.

Dustin is sitting in the corner when I go to pick him up from after-school care. He looks mad. On the other side of the room sits another sour-looking kid.

Not again.

Mrs. Ford, the lady in charge, zips over. She's easily as fast as any fourth grader. "Dan," she begins, "I'm afraid Dustin's had some trouble this afternoon."

I eye my little brother, who looks away, suddenly interested in the kids at the playdough table. "Let me guess — fighting?"

"I'm afraid so." Mrs. Ford looks very sorry. "He's such an angry boy. Is everything okay at home?"

26

"Fine," I say. "I think it's a growth spurt. It won't happen again."

She bobs her head. "I'm glad to hear that. However ... "

"I know, I know."

" ... fighting is not tolerated in our program. We've let Dustin off a few times, but I'm afraid he's used his last warning. I'm going to have to suspend him."

"So how do I —" I begin to ask.

"You can pick him up from the school office. He can stay there up to fifteen minutes after the bell rings." She lays a hand on my arm. "I'm sorry, Dan. Rules are rules."

Dustin is silent as he grabs his pack and we head for home. It's warm outside, an Indian summer. We each carry our jackets over one arm, sweat forming under our backpacks. Snow isn't far off, but this afternoon, it feels like August. Dustin stops to stuff his coat into his backpack. "You were late," he mutters.

"So you decided to take it out on your buddy there?" I ask.

Dustin shrugs and we start walking again, crossing in front of Gupta's Grocery, owned by Chain's family. Inside the propped-open door, I can see Chain next to the candy bars. He's talking up a tall East Indian girl with long black hair and a careful smile. I recognize her as Padma, the girl Chain's been chasing after since the beginning of the year.

"Hey, Nutbar!" Chain yells, spotting me.

Dustin grabs my hand. I give it a squeeze and let go. "What's up, Chain?"

He struts out of the store, looking like a fighting cock, and stops in front of me, blocking the sidewalk. His body spray attacks me before he's even had the chance to. It's a train wreck of sharp citrus and heavily-spiced perfume — probably called Smells Like Teen Jerk.

"Do me a favour." Chain sneers, making sure Padma gets a good look at his superiority. "Keep your mom out of my store."

"Why?"

"Because she's a whack job. She was telling my grandma about some stupid numbers this afternoon. Said they were supposed to bring bad luck or something." Chain drops his voice. "Grandma thinks it's an omen. She's completely freaked out. All I know is if your mom comes in here again, I'm calling the cops."

"You can't call the cops just because someone says your grandma's going to have bad luck."

"Yeah, well, Grandma's too scared to run the store now. My dad made me take her shift."

I shrug, "So my mom got you a job. What's the big deal?"

Chain lunges, furious. He holds his fist to my face. "I swear I'm going to make your life miserable until my grandma takes her job back."

"Have fun with that." I smile, grabbing Dustin by the arm and pulling him around Chain.

Chain yells behind us, "Your whole family's crazy! I hope they sell tiny straitjackets for your brother."

I turn back, my breath coming hard. "At least I don't live above a crappy old store!"

"At least I don't have an insane mom!" he yells back.

I light up a sneering grin. "At least I don't have to go to work right now."

Chain jumps at me, his fists raised. I turn and run just as his dad calls him inside with sharp Punjabi.

"I hate that guy," Dustin says when we're on the next block.

"Don't worry about him."

Dustin looks at his feet. "It's hard."

I squeeze his shoulder. "Yeah, it's hard to ignore jerks. But you've got to. I mean, we have enough to deal with. Right?"

"I guess."

Our apartment finally comes into view half a block away. "So who was that kid you were fighting with at school?" I ask.

"Doesn't matter." Dustin mumbles something else. Something familiar.

"What?" I feel as though I just swallowed a tub of ice water.

"I said he's a stupid seven!" Dustin repeats, his voice clipped.

My reaction is so immediate I even take myself by surprise. I have Dustin by the front of his shirt, pressed hard against the brick wall of the neighbouring apartment building, my breath coming in gasps. "Don't," I say, my words tight. "Don't ever do that. Mom's numbers are just for her. Only her!" I shove him again, my fist thumping his chest. "Got it?"

He glares back, tears forming in his big brown eyes.

I loosen my grip, my hands shaking as much as my voice. "Never again."

"Okay!" Dustin pulls away and runs down the sidewalk to our apartment building.

I see him waiting, peering inside, hoping someone will come out so he doesn't have to wait for me to unlock the door. Our building's caretaker, who I am sure is an ex-KGB spy, finally lets Dustin in. I catch up with him on the second floor, outside the door to our apartment. His eyes are big and worried. His anger has vanished.

"Mom's home," he says so softly he may as well be mouthing it.

I frown and check the time. She's not supposed to be home yet. Work doesn't end for at least half an hour. "Don't worry. It'll be okay," I whisper back.

"The sevens don't lie." Her voice is clear. So is the thumping of her feet as she stalks the apartment. "He's ... he's a betrayer! Gotta be!" Something smashes. Sounds like glass. Mom's going downhill faster than usual. Maybe she'll spiral up just as fast.

Fingers crossed.

Chapter 6

Supper over, Dustin watches SpongeBob while Mom hides in her room doing more drawings and muttering numbers to herself. I try to get her to take the last remaining pill and ask if she's picked up her prescription yet. She just waves me off and closes her bedroom door, her voice drifting through the wood: "I'm fine, Daniel. I don't need that poison anymore."

I retrieve my backpack from where I hid it in the hall outside our apartment. There was no need to let Mom in on the fact that I went to school. The pictures Mom was drawing last night have been taped to the walls around the living room and charms have been placed on all the doors and cupboards. It's kind of creepy.

My room is crazy-poster free, so I retreat there and get to work on my English assignment. We're supposed to analyze some rap song. In theory this is supposed to make us feel that the teacher actually cares about what we like. I call Heather to see if I'm even doing the assignment right.

"We don't do rap in my English class," she says. "We do sonnets by Shakespeare."

I huff out a breath. "Well that sucks. Do you even listen to rap?"

"Umm," she says, a sarcastic edge to her voice, "I'm an aspiring metal queen."

"Oh, right."

"Speaking of which … "

"Speaking of what?" I ask, already knowing where this is heading.

"Any decision?"

"I still don't know if I'm being expelled."

"You were in school this afternoon and no one came after you."

"Administration can take time."

"Come on, Dan. What are you so scared of? It's just for fun."

"And … " I know there's more. "You want me because … ?"

"You're the only bassist I know," she says softly.

"That sounds more like it," I chuckle.

"But you're nice. And . . ." she pauses, "cute."

My heart stops for a millisecond, like a sneeze. I may have just died. I check my pulse. Still beating.

"Dan?"

"I … um … I'll think about it."

"For real?"

All my previous objections fly from my brain.

Me and Heather. Together. Cool. "Yeah."

"Okay. See you at school tomorrow. Good luck with the rap."

"Right, rap." Rap is the last thing on my mind.

I end up writing down a bunch of random things in my notebook that probably have nothing to do with the song. My brain will not focus after talking with Heather. It's not until I grab my bass and throw on my headphones to keep the noise from the amp down that I feel like myself again.

I love my bass. It's a matte blue and has a few scars and scratches, but that just makes it more awesome. I play a riff I've been working on for a while, then grab my MP3 player and put the earbuds under the puffy headphones. This way I can play along with my favourite songs. I've been working on Pantera's "Cowboys From Hell" lately. I'm trying to learn more metal. It's coming along great. I wonder what Heather would think.

I want to join her band so bad. It would be fun — and fun is something I need in my life. Muttering mothers and little brothers who want to play number games just don't cut it. Still, I can't think of how to swing the whole band thing. I doubt her parents would be cool about letting us play at eleven at night. Really, that's my only free time. When everyone is in bed and asleep and I can sneak out.

But there's got to be a way. I'll have to work on it.

I look at the clock. It's already eight forty-five.

I go see if Mom has Dustin in bed. As usual, he's still glued to the TV, his nose inches away from the screen, and Mom is nowhere in sight. This isn't fair.

"Hey, kid." I shake his shoulder, trying to retrieve him from zombieland. "Come on, bedtime."

"Aww," he whines. "This show just started! It's about ghosts. It's cool."

I check the guide. "It didn't just start. It's been on for forty-five minutes."

"So?" he says stubbornly, not looking at me. "It's almost over."

"Not for another hour and a quarter," I reason.

"Who cares?"

"No more ghosts tonight." I touch his shoulder gently.

He pulls away. "Nuh uh. I'm watching."

I try to keep my voice level. "You were almost late for school today. I need to be on time tomorrow. Early even. Come on, bedtime."

He crosses his arms. Pushes his face closer to the screen. Blocks me out of his view. "You're not Mom. You can't tell me what to do."

All my frustration at having to deal with my mother's responsibilities comes out in one insane moment. I grab his shoulder and shove his head into the screen — hard. "There," I growl low enough not to alert Mom. "You want to watch TV? Watch the stupid thing."

The TV wobbles and tips backward, hitting the wall with a thud. Dustin flings his arms out and runs to his room, his face twisting with oncoming sobs. I right the TV on its stand and turn it off. Already I'm feeling guilty. Maybe Chain is right. Maybe I am a schizo-nutbar. Schizophrenia starts showing up in the late teens and it's genetic too. Maybe I'm going to end up as crazy as my mom.

My whole body shaking, I collapse onto the couch. Today has been too much. Between Dustin, Mom, Chain, and Heather, I have every emotion bouncing around inside me. I grab my head with my hands. Pressure builds in my chest. Wetness coats my palms. A sniffle and gulp escape. I fight down the feeling of illness and dread. Then, with a deep breath, wipe my eyes and get up, tripping over Dustin's stuffed dog that he dropped when he ran away. I pick it up and hug it.

By the time I get to Dustin's room, he's already in bed. He has the covers pulled over his head and his bedroom lights are out. "Dustin?" I call.

His hand snakes out and turns on his lamp. "What?" he asks, his voice sullen and raw.

"Sorry." I put the dog in his hand.

"Thanks." He throws back the covers. His forehead is red but not bleeding. I don't even think there's going to be a bruise. The knots in my gut start to untwist.

"I'll get up early," he says.

"Okay." I go to leave.

"Dan?"

"What?"

"Tell me our story."

Exhaustion washes over me. It's been a hell of a day. I don't think I can do one more thing. "Not tonight."

"Please?" Dustin rubs his forehead, making another rush of guilt run through me.

"Fine," I sigh. "From what part?"

"All of it. From the beginning. From you."

Chapter 7

"All the way back to me? My beginning?" I shake my head. "It's already past your bedtime."

"Dan..." Dustin whines.

I let out a long breath. I guess I owe him after slamming him into the TV. "Fine." I go back to his bed and sit on the edge. He snuggles next to me, head on his pillow, eyes smiling.

Our story, as Dustin calls it, is the closest thing to a fairy tale we have. And it has all the good parts of a traditional fairy tale — murder, betrayal, love. It's his favourite story, even though I've tried a number of times to distract him with books about aliens, mummies, and race cars. No luck, he likes the story about us.

"Okay, so when Mom was about sixteen —"

"You forgot the beginning." Dustin grins, hugging his stuffed dog tight and looking pleased.

I grind my teeth, smile, and start again. "Once

upon a time there was a girl named Denise. She was sixteen and hunting for a man."

That was the way my mom told me — hunting for a man. I never knew women classified men as prey. Then again, remembering Heather trying to get me into her band today, Mom may be right.

"The man's name was Cameron."

"A three seven," Dustin chimes in with Mom's number code.

I give him a warning look.

"Sorry," he says.

"That was when the numbers where just getting started. They weren't as powerful back then. She could date a three seven and not have problems. Or so she thought. Cameron was sweet and kind and gave her lots of things."

"Like necklaces and shoes," Dustin murmurs, his eyelids starting to droop.

"Yeah." I smile. "Like necklaces and shoes. Mom liked Cameron so much that they got really close and she got pregnant."

"But Cameron was a betrayer."

"Who's telling this story?" I ask, giving him a playful shove.

"Sorry." He smiles.

"Cameron was five years older than Mom and married with kids of his own. He didn't want anyone to know about the affair he was having with our mother. So instead of helping her out, he moved with his family and disappeared, never to be seen again."

"And you never saw your dad."

"Never. After that the numbers started getting stronger. They began to show their power. Mom thought it was because she broke the rules by going out with Cameron and she tried to kill herself."

"But Grandma and Aunt Clara stopped her."

"Yes, they did."

"And you were born." Dustin squeezes my hand.

"Lucky for you," I say, before continuing. "Mom and I lived with Grandma and Aunt Clara for a long time, until I was just starting kindergarten. They helped take care of me, especially when Mom had her bad days. But in secret, Mom taught me how to do the calculations. She showed me how to keep the evil at bay."

Dustin's eyes grow wide. I always like to make this part sound ominous, but sometimes I worry. "It's just a story. You know that, right?"

He nods. "The numbers aren't real. Tell my part."

"Okay. One day the numbers mounted a campaign and took over Mom's mind. She was sent to the hospital to get better."

"And she did get better."

"Yes, she did. And she also met Dice while she was there."

"A four four."

"Double good numbers. Dice was in the hospital because he was sad too much. They fell in love. When they both got out, they moved in together. Grandma and Aunt Clara didn't think it was a good idea, but Dice kept Mom from being scared of numbers all the time, so they had to let it go."

"He was from Jamaica," Dustin says, yawning.

"He was, but he couldn't go back. His family always made him cry. Mom and Dice got married and soon you were growing inside her. Those were the best times in the world. Mom was happy and she made Dice happy — he was hardly ever sad in those days. Dice even taught me how to play his blue bass."

"Your blue bass."

"It was his back then. When you were born, we were like a normal family. There were no numbers. Well ... the numbers were a lot less."

"Because Dice made sure Mom took her pills."

"Yeah," I nod. "We went on picnics and played soccer and did all kinds of stuff like every other family."

"Then we went to Hawaii."

"When you were two, we took a trip to Hawaii. It was so hot and the beaches were so white. I remember playing in the ocean and building a sandcastle all around you. You thought you were a king."

"Then when we got back ... "

"Gloom descended. A big dark cloud came crashing down. Dice tried to avoid it. He tried to work hard to beat it but the gloom was just too strong and it covered him with sadness."

"Then you found him."

"I found him hanging from the dining room light with a belt around his neck when I got home from school. You were in daycare. Mom was at work. I was nine. Same age as you are now."

"You were scared."

I swallow and keep going. "When Mom saw the paramedics with Dice, her wall against the numbers cracked. The numbers came sneaking back in. Grandma and Aunt Clara wanted to take us to live with them until Mom felt better … "

"But that's how she knew."

"Yes, that's how she knew that the gloom had been unleashed by Aunt Clara and Grandma in order to get rid of Dice and capture us. They were traitors. Betrayers. So, to keep us safe, Mom hid and never spoke to them again."

"But she still battles the numbers."

"Every single day."

"And now you make her take her pills."

"I try."

Dustin blinks, then squints. "Do you think she'll ever get happy again like she did in Hawaii?"

I shrug. "I hope so. We're under a cloud of gloom right now, aren't we?"

Dustin nods. "But you'll keep me safe."

"Always. You're my brother. Now," I pat his back and turn out the lamp, "get some sleep. You have to get up early tomorrow."

"Okay."

Dustin snuggles down into his covers and I

41

quietly close the door behind me. I press my ear to the hollow wood of Mom's door. Not a sound. Maybe she's asleep. I can only hope. Just a little while longer and I can have a little R and R time for myself.

Chapter 8

By eleven o'clock, I'm sitting in a dark corner of the Night Owl Café drinking coffee. The Night Owl is hidden in the basement of a downtown historical building, complete with carved stone roses and wide marble staircases. It's a favourite hangout of street kids and the university dropout set. It's dark, it's weird, and it has awesome jam sessions. I only played once, but it was great. I just never seem to have the energy to sneak my bass guitar out of the apartment. And I'm too worried about being jumped and getting it stolen on my way home.

People often draw and paint at the tables and any artwork not taken home gets thumbtacked to the wall. That, and any items left behind that aren't totally disgusting or illegal. The latest creations include a picture of a naked girl done in blue finger paint and a doll's head magic-markered to look like Marilyn Manson. They have the best old-school punk music blasting over the sound system, like the Circle Jerks, D.O.A., Suicidal Tendencies, and The Exploited. And even though the Night Owl only opened in the spring, it's quickly become my favourite hangout. Trust me, it's much better than walking around freezing my butt off just to get some alone time. There's not a lot of people here tonight, but given the size of the room, they pretty much fill the space. Most don't order more than coffee, even though they also sell kickass veggie sandwiches. Hardly anyone has much money. I just can't see this place lasting.

Gordon, the owner of the café, strolls past smelling of Playboy cologne and pot. "Jam session Thursday night. Bring your bass if you're interested," he says in his lazy monotone, laying down a flyer before moving on.

"You should play," Tracy says, pulling up a chair across from me. Tracy has a frizzy purple mohawk, her skin is pale, and her eyes are light blue. I have a feeling she's really a blond under the hair dye, but who knows. She's thin and short and still has an innocent look. Not bad for being on the street nearly a year.

I bump fists with her before flipping over the flyer so I can't see it. "Nah."

She points to the bags under my eyes. "Not sleeping again?"

"Sleeping is for wimps," I reply.

"Amen to that." Tracy raises her skinny arms

like a southern Baptist minister and shakes her head. "We are not wimps. Need another therapy session?" she laughs.

"How much is it going to cost me?"

"The usual — a coffee."

I get up and buy her a cup of java — not as payment, but because Tracy is my confidante. The only one I've ever really opened up to about my mom's schizophrenia. Tracy caught me at a moment of weakness, wandering around downtown. Crying. She grabbed my hand and plonked me on a cold metal bench, bus fumes belching all around us. She had me telling her my problems until nearly midnight before she really introduced herself. It was weird, meeting this cute, purple-mohawked girl in the middle of the night and letting out my secrets. I guess I couldn't keep it inside any longer. All that pain and confusion would have broken out eventually. I'm just glad it happened with Tracy.

Tracy's a good listener. Everyone here knows it, too. She generally has at least one or two people around her ready to launch into their problems. I think it makes her happy to be needed. In turn, all us whiners buy her coffee and sandwiches and stuff. It keeps her out of trouble with the police — for the most part, anyway.

She sure hadn't felt needed at home — more like an accessory for her mom, like a bracelet or new pair of shoes, and an employee to her dad, someone to follow his rules or be fired. She left home last Christmas. I think she was hoping her parents would freak out and beg her to come back. Nothing like that happened, but she's still hoping.

"So what's up?" Tracy asks, tipping her head to the side. "Your mom still losing it?"

I shrug. "You know. She's back to drawing posters."

"Ahh, art class begins," Tracy smiles. "That's not so bad. Nothing you haven't survived before."

I draw a deep breath, bringing with it the taste of fresh baked bread, coffee, and human funk. "You're right. I can deal. I just don't like Dustin being so scared."

"He has you."

"Yup. Always," I say, just as Farmer launches himself across the room and leaps into the chair between us, knocking into me.

"Did she tell you?" he asks. There's so much energy around him that his body seems like it's vibrating. His long brown hair flies as he twists his head to look at us both.

Farmer's a kid who hitched into Calgary this summer hoping to make it big with his music. So far he and his band don't do much more than play covers and get stoned, but that hasn't dampened their spirits. He's also way too hyper. I'm not sure if it's too many drugs or not enough of the right kind.

"Tell me what?" I ask, eyeing Tracy.

She beams. "Farmer hooked me up with a place to stay. It's sweet."

I raise an eyebrow. There's nothing sweet on the street that doesn't come with a nasty price. "So where is this sweet place?"

"Not too far from here. It's a closet."

"A closet?" I ask.

"It's true," Farmer says nodding. "Our girl lives in a closet, and now she's out." He laughs till he chokes.

"Shut up," Tracy says, annoyed but still grinning.

Farmer's eyes scan the room, stopping when they hit Carl, a kid from the Siksika reserve who makes Chain look like an underfed midget. "Gotta jet, boys and girls," Farmer announces. "This guy owes me money." He leaps out of his chair, dodging random people and jumping on Carl's back, making him twist and squirm to see who's landed on him.

"Farmer's so strange," Tracy says.

"So you're staying in a closet?" I ask, thinking of a tiny dark space with folding doors. "How do you fit?"

"It's a walk-in closet in an old apartment building. It even has a window. A lady that Farmer met offered it to me until I get off the street."

"So she's just letting you stay there? For free? Come on."

Tracy shrugs. "I know, eh?"

There is no one that just helps people for free. No one that I've ever heard of. "So, what is she, a social worker?" I ask.

"No, she works at a used clothing store."

"Is she nuts?"

"No. Just someone who wants to help."

I shake my head. It can't be that simple. Nothing is that simple. "So this lady, she took you in, let you stay in her closet ... "

"Yeah, the living room was full. Farmer and his band live there. Basically the closet was the only place left in the apartment."

"Right ... What does she get out of it?"

Tracy shrugs. "I don't know. She hooked me up with this youth outreach group, though. This social worker, Brian, says he can help me get back together with my parents. Cool, huh?"

I frown. I think Tracy is oversimplifying things. "Are you sure you want to?"

Tracy runs her hand through her hair, tugging distractedly. "I don't want to be homeless forever and it would be nice to find out if they miss me."

"Are you scared?"

A clump of hair comes out in her hand. She looks at the lifeless purple frizz in her palm. "I think I've overdone it with the hair dye. Maybe I should just shave my hair off. Mommy and Daddy definitely won't approve of the mohawk. Though," she rolls her eyes up toward the ceiling, "they should be happy just to have me back. Don't you think?"

I watch the hopeful expression flitting over her pale skin and nod. "They would have to be stupid to not want you back, mohawked or not."

"That reminds me." Tracy reaches into her pocket. "I have something for you." She pulls out a lined sheet of paper with a ballpoint-pen drawing on it.

I take it and smooth it out on the table. "It's a picture of you," I say, looking at the obvious likeness. "You draw it?"

"Nah, I can't draw. Detroit did it last night. I wanted you to have it, in case ... "

"In case what?"

"Well, if this thing with my parents doesn't work out, I'm going to Vancouver. I have an aunt there. My dad hates her, so she must be cool. I'm going to see if I can hang out with her. "

"And if that doesn't work out?"

She shrugs.

I shudder. Girls like Tracy go to Vancouver all the time. Not too many come back.

"If she does let me stay with her, maybe you can come live with us too. It would be fun." Tracy smiles.

"But I can't leave D—" I begin to say when Tracy suddenly jumps up, all smiles, to meet the people coming down the stairs. "Alex! Detroit! How'd it go?"

Alex and Detroit soon have their jackets off — chains clinking, hot coffee in hand — and are telling us in slapstick detail about their night's adventures. And I love it. I love the normality of hanging out. Being with friends. Not having to worry about who my mom's been scaring, or if my little brother gets to bed on time, or even how many classes I've slept through.

Three coffees later, I glance at the Gene Simmons clock behind the counter and decide two in the morning is a good time to shut this party down. After saying goodbye to everyone, I head out into the night. The warm afternoon air has been replaced by small, prickly snowflakes sliding in on a northern wind. Winter is definitely coming.

By the time I get to the apartment building's big front door, I'm completely frozen and more exhausted than ever. I consider skipping school entirely tomorrow. It's going to be hard to go anyway, with Mom growing ever more convinced that my school is the root of all evil. Besides, there's no way in hell she's going to write a cheque for my fees, so what's the point? I grab the elevator to the second floor and pull out my key. The thing is, school isn't so bad. It's normal, and I like normal. And Heather is there …

I need a plan. I need a cheque. I'll have to think of something.

Chapter 9

It's amazing what a celery stick will do for the brain cells. Between sneaking into the darkened apartment and hitting the refrigerator, I came up with an idea. The fan on my laptop whirs as I open a blank document and pull up the school's website. Grabbing a sheet of paper, I write out the alphabet and number each letter, fire up my calculator, and get ready to use math to balance my mom's universe.

Numbers. Our life has always been about numbers. Every word falls into this system. For example, my mom's name — Denise — starts with the fourth letter of the alphabet and there are six letters in the word. Therefore, she is a four six. Being a four six makes her sacred, ordered, and safe. At least according to her system.

I'm a four six too. Dustin as well. Can you guess who named us? It's one of the reasons I prefer the name Dan to Daniel. Her numbers drive me crazy. But if I use them right, I can get what I want. And right now I want to get the principal, Mr. Garnnet, off my back.

Copying and pasting, I steal the Calgary Board of Education's logo. In seconds, I have a new, safe name for both the school and the principal. Surfing images, I find something that will make a great logo for our newly-named school and paste that in, too. Then I take the note about the school fees out of my backpack and copy it, changing things as needed. Finally, I track down an illegible scrawl and ... Done! One new letter asking for school fees at the *Lighting the Future High School* signed by *Doctor Devlin*.

Lighting the Future High School. I smile. It's perfect. Lighting is a twelve eight which in Mom's world really means three fours and two fours. Oh crap. That makes it five fours, which might not be good. Fives are bad right now. I wonder if she'll pick that up.

I yawn and look at the clock. It's three in the morning. I need sleep and I'm too tired to do this anymore. It will have to do. The printer spits out my new letter, which I shove into an envelope, seal, then rip open again so it looks like I got it from someone else. Then I shut everything down and crawl into bed. My fingers are crossed that she buys it.

Chapter 10

"I know you snuck out last night," Dustin says.

We're rushing. It's already ten in the morning. In my overtired state I forgot to set the alarm clock. As a result, I'm late again. Story of my life. It's colder this morning than it has been so far this fall. The sky is overcast and dim. Small snowflakes drift down in the gusting wind.

Dustin is upset. It seems he has some kind of hip-hop presentation this morning and he's sure he's already missed it. On the plus side, I managed to get not only one but four signed cheques from Mom before we left, all of them blank. She seemed to think that because the letter had so many good fours in it, four cheques were required. I guess that means I get to buy the new Converse high-tops I've had my eye on. According to Mom, Converse is an evil brand and shouldn't be worn. I have no issue with having evil feet.

"I know you snuck out last night," Dustin repeats.

"What are you talking about?" I ask, playing dumb.

Dustin smiles slyly, pushing his skateboard with one foot, his shoes already soaked. "I know you go out at night."

"When?"

"Sometimes. After Mom and me go to bed."

I shake my head. "No."

He punches me. "Don't lie. I woke up to go to the bathroom and then I went to sleep in your bed, except you weren't there. Mom was home, but you weren't."

Dustin tries to kickflip his board. I grab his shoulder to keep him from flipping himself. "I just went down to the lobby," I say, "to check the mail."

"Nuh uh. You went out."

"Where would I go in the middle of the night?"

Dustin shrugs. "I don't know. You still did it. But what if … "

"What if what?"

"What if Mom wakes up when you're gone?"

"Has that ever happened?" I mentally cross my fingers and hope he doesn't realize it has.

"No."

I let out the breath I've been holding. "Dustin," I say, listening to the clicking of his skateboard as it goes over the gaps in the sidewalk. "I won't let anything bad happen to you."

"But what if you're not there?"

"I'm always there."

Lying to my brother feels so wrong. But I *deserve* to go out. I *deserve* to act like every other kid on the face of the planet. I'm not his parent anyway. So what's the big deal?

I drop Dustin off in the office and remind him to wait for me there after school. At my school I also go straight to the office. I've missed my first class again. The least I can do is pay my school fees. Mr. Garnnet walks by while I'm leaning against the counter, waiting for a receipt.

"Daniel ... "

"Dan," I correct him.

"Right, Dan. You're late again."

"Just following your suggestion, sir," I say, hoping my many lies aren't about to catch up with me. "I was getting more sleep."

Mr. Garnnet laughs. "I think you should maybe shift your extra sleep to earlier in the night. School is just as important."

"I'll keep that in mind." I grab my receipt from the secretary just as the bell rings. I fight my way through the crowded hallway to my locker and check my day two schedule. Social Studies second period. Joy. I skip the math book and actually grab my social studies text. Heather is smiling at me when I slip into my desk.

"So," she says. "You're not suspended."

I haven't quite come up with a plan that could get Dustin and me out of the house without my

55

mom slipping into total paranoia. It sucks. This is why I only go out when she's either at work or asleep. But there's got to be a way. Like planting decoy sounds in my bedroom to make her believe Dustin and I are hanging out in there. It might work.

"I'm still thinking about it."

"Come on." Heather frowns. "I told you, your brother can play with mine. It will be fun for both of you. What's your holdup?"

She flips her hair over her shoulder and looks me straight in the eye. Every part of me wants to give in to her and say yes. It would be like the Night Owl without the sleep deprivation. But I shake my head. "It's complicated."

"Complicated how? Your mom ground you or something?"

I chuckle. "No. Not that. Just complicated."

"What?" Heather persists. "Is she super mean?"

"Not exactly." I sigh. "It's just … complicated. My mom is … "

I'm so busy thinking of an explanation that will keep Heather happy and not dig me into a hole I can't climb out of that I don't notice Chain until he's nailed me in the shoulder. The pain is blinding. I grab my arm and glare at him.

"His mom is nuts," he tells Heather. "Cuckoo. Needs a straitjacket." Chain wraps his fist in the fabric of my shirt and hauls me half out of my seat. "By the way," he says, breath sour on my face, "that's for my grandma. Expect one every day until I don't have to run the store anymore."

The start-of-class bell rings and Chain shoves me back against the desk before moving toward his friends. Heather raises her eyebrow in a silent question as the teacher arrives. I look away from her and end up staring straight at Mr. Johnston. He scowls at me like he knows I've been late again. Man, I hope I'm not the talk of the teacher's lounge. Seriously, does every day have to be so messed up?

Chapter 11

When we get home from school, Dustin drops his backpack in the middle of the floor and throws himself onto the couch. He grabs the remote and turns on SpongeBob, volume amped. I know he's trying to drown out Mom's chanting coming from the bedroom. She's home early again, second day in a row, and there are new pictures taped to the wall — numbers around buildings, and hollow people with swirling designs filling them in.

Mom sounds bad. Worse than I've ever heard her before. I go to get her medication and find the last pill, the blister pack, and the box crushed on the kitchen counter. Mom has written fives and sevens on the mangled pack. I wish I knew what to do. Had someone to call. The phone rings. I pick it up. It's Daphne, Mom's friend from work. Dustin and I met her at the company Christmas party last year. If she's calling, there must be more trouble.

"What's up, Daphne?" I ask, trying to sound chipper.

"Is your mom there?" She's hissing into the phone. It sounds like she's trying to keep everyone, including me, from hearing the conversation.

"She's busy at the moment," I answer at a normal volume. "Can I take a message?"

"I think your mom did something to the data system. Management is investigating *right now*. She'd better think of a good excuse before she comes in tomorrow or she's going to lose her job."

"I'll let her know," I say, knowing I'll do no such thing. I'm not getting caught in the middle of this.

"What's going on with her?" Daphne whispers, still keeping her voice barely audible. "Your mom left early again and she was acting really strange. I always thought she was a bit eccentric but . . ."

"She's fine. She had a dentist appointment this afternoon," I say. Lying's getting to be a habit.

Daphne gives a nervous laugh. "Oh," she says, sounding slightly embarrassed, "that explains everything. I hate dentists too. Makes me freak out every time."

I smile and know the office gossip may just save my mom her job. "Well, I'm glad we got that cleared up. Nice talking to you Daphne, but I have homework and ... yeah."

"Oh, for sure. Nice talking to you too, Daniel."

"It's Dan," I say under my breath.

I hang up just as Mom starts yelling "five,

seven, five, seven," over and over. Dustin cranks the volume on the TV and Mr. Jones bangs on the wall. I go to the kitchen and open the junk drawer.

In the drawer, along with half a wireless mouse, parts for recharging a cordless phone, pizza menus from places that have long since gone out of business, bottle caps with codes for contests concluded at least three years ago, eight thousand elastic bands tangled up with two million bread ties — is a small address book.

I find it way at the back, under a palm tree key chain from Hawaii. For a second I hold the key chain tightly in my hand and think of Dice. He made Mom so happy she hardly counted at all. He was able to keep her taking her pills, even though she hated it. He kept both Dustin and me safe and normal.

Anger blooms inside my chest, like blood in water. Why did he have to kill himself? Why did he leave us alone, *me* alone, to deal with this? Why was he so selfish? So sick? So sad?

I shove the key chain back into the drawer and pull out the phone book. It's really small, about the size of a pack of gum. On its cover is an orange kitten playing with a ball of yarn. Inside are phone numbers for Grandma and my aunt Clara. I don't even know if they're right anymore. I run my finger over the numbers, wondering just what would happen if I called. Would they reject me the way Mom rejected them? Would they help? And how would they do that? By taking us away from her?

By calling in Social Services? From what Tracy and has said, Social Services would split me and Dustin up. Make everything worse. But I don't know that for sure. She could be wrong.

Mom starts crying. Long, sobbing gulps that echo down the hallway. What would happen to her if I called? She'd probably be locked up. Drugged with pills she believes are poison. Would she think it was all my fault?

I snap the book closed. I can't do that to Mom right now. Not when she's so scared. Not when her world is attacking her. Sliding the address book into my back pocket, I begin to make supper. Maybe Mom will feel better tomorrow.

Chapter 12

"Up," I tell Dustin, shaking his shoulder. His room is dim from the calculation-covered sheets of paper that line his walls and windows. "I'm grabbing a shower. You better be dressed by the time I get back. I'm not going to be late again." I actually feel good. Maybe it helped that I went to bed the same time as Dustin. I can only live on minimal sleep for so long.

I wake my mom up on the way to the bathroom. Her face is a mess of graphite streaks from her black-smudged fingers. Pencils lie all over her room, most of them broken in half. Papers cover every wall, hung with packing tape and filled with numbers. She looks at me, disoriented, like she's not quite here. Like she's seeing another world. "Come on, Mom," I say, before closing her bedroom door. "It's a new day."

The shower is refreshing. The water drowns

out all the morning noises and the heat loosens my knotted muscles. I think today I'm going to tell Heather I can jam with her band. Just for today. What harm can one afternoon do? It would make Heather happy, and maybe even earn me another kiss. And as long as Mom is either at work or calculating in her room, what does she care if I slip out for a few hours?

By the time I'm ready for school, both Mom and Dustin are at the table. Mom has on her work clothes and the graphite streaks on her face have been replaced by makeup. Dustin is dressed too, wearing his jeans and favourite SpongeBob hoodie. He looks freaked. Mom is doing something to his arm. When I move to the other side of the table, I can see she has Dustin's wrist in a tight grip. She's writing numbers on his skin with a permanent marker. Dustin looks like he's ready to cry. I touch his shoulder.

"What are you doing?" I ask, trying to keep my voice casual.

"The code is crumbling," Mom mutters, deep in concentration. "The numbers won't sparkle. They're getting angry and dark. I need to protect you both. I need to keep you safe."

"We are safe," I try to reason with her. "Dustin doesn't need the tattoo."

She turns on me so fast her chair flips over. The marker is pointed inches from my nose. Dustin covers his arm with his sleeve and scoots under the table. "What do you know about it?" she shrieks.

"I know that ink from a Sharpie isn't going to save him from being hit by a car or teased at school."

"You know nothing about this!" Mom looks at me suspiciously. "Maybe..." She narrows her eyes. "Maybe it's you. Maybe you're the one doing all this."

"How?" I ask, getting angry. "None of it's real." I hate seeing Dustin scared. I hate having to hide, sweet-talk, and lie just to get through a day. I hate this life! I feel the hard edges of the address book in my pocket. "Maybe... maybe it's time to get help."

"Help?" she screams, her face turning red. "Help from where?"

"Grandma?" I ask, my voice slipping into squeaky uncertainty.

"You have been infiltrated!" Mom announces.

"Infiltrated by what?" I demand.

"I got an automated call about you missing class yesterday. They haven't changed the name of the school at all. You lied. They made you lie. They're warping your mind."

I ball my fists. Feel spit fly from my mouth. "They didn't do anything. I *want* to go to school."

"They're going to hurt you."

"The only one that's going to hurt me is Chain Gupta and only because you're crazy!" I grab Dustin from under the table and pull him out, snagging his coat and backpack from beside his chair. "Come on, let's go to school."

Mom grabs Dustin's other arm. "No! I have to take him! I have to make sure he stays safe!"

"Owww!" Dustin howls as we each pull an arm. "Let me go!"

Like an electric jolt, I realize what I'm doing and drop his arm. Mom still clings to him.

Chapter 13

Dustin's calmed down by the time I get him to school.

"You'll pick me up?" he asks, rubbing his hand over his jacket sleeve. It's the arm Mom markered up.

"I promise. Right after school."

"Are you going out tonight?" His eyes are still a little red, like he's holding in the pain and fear.

"I told you, I don't sneak out."

"But if you were going to ..."

"I'm not. I'll be home."

"But what if —"

"Dustin," I take his hand in mine and give it a squeeze. "I promise you'll be safe."

"But what if —"

"No more what ifs." I pull a half-finished pack of orange Tic Tacs out of my pocket and hand it to him. "Here, candy. Now cheer up. You're going to have a good day. Don't you have an assembly or something?"

"That was yesterday."

"Right." I feel completely disoriented. "You'll be safe. Now get going."

He nods and lopes to the playground. I watch him for a few seconds before grabbing my bus and heading to school.

I managed to get Dustin free from Mom's grip by swearing I'd come home right after dropping him off. Of course, I have no intention of doing that. I need to see Heather. I even need to see Chain. I just need some normal.

I get to Western Canada High fifteen minutes before the bell. I take my time at my locker and check my day three schedule. Math, period one. Slowly, I make my way toward my classroom.

"Dan," a voice calls out.

I spin and look. Mr. Garnnet is striding through the masses, waving.

"You look rested," he says, smiling. "I see you took my advice."

"Yup. Going to sleep early, who knew?"

"Getting to class on time," Mr. Garnnet says, his eyes crinkling in a smile. "Must be a good feeling."

Just being here, with normal kids doing normal stuff, is a good feeling. I wonder, sometimes, if anyone else has a life like mine. I've never heard of it. Not once.

"Well, have a great day," Mr. Garnnet says,

heading off down the hall. I spot Heather by the classroom door. We have Math together. Seeing her face is the only thing that makes it bearable. I have a real aversion to numbers.

"Hey Heather," I say, smiling. "I'll jam with you after school today."

Her face lights up, then falls. "Sorry Dan, my dad's in town tonight. I have to go out to dinner."

"Tomorrow?" I ask.

She looks unhappy. "Sebastian has something tomorrow. We're jamming on Friday though. Can you come then?"

Friday, I think. I can do Friday. Really, what's the difference? "Okay."

Heather cheers and gives me a quick hug that leaves me feeling faint. "I'm going to text Maggie and Sebastian. They'll freak."

She moves away, punching her phone with her thumbs. Trying to get it done before the bell rings. I watch her, my brain mush. Chain's fist slamming into my shoulder brings me back to reality.

"Day two, Nutbar," he sneers. "It's kind of hard to hang out with Padma when I don't have after-noons off. But you wouldn't know anything about that, would you, Nutbar? Your crazy mother lets you do whatever you want."

I want to yell. Tell Chain that my life is way more complicated than anyone knows. But what would he say? That I was lying? That I deserve it? He would call me a loser for going along with Mom's illusions.

Well, I'm not playing her games today. And I'm not going to feel guilty about calling her crazy either — that's something I've never done before, not to her face anyway. I've had enough. I'm here. At school. Getting beat up. Yeah, normal.

Chapter 14

After school, I have my ear to the apartment door. I'm breathing in old varnish and dead skin cells while listening to see what's going on inside. I hear nothing. I twist the doorknob and find it locked. I give Dustin the thumbs-up. He smiles back. Mom must be at work.

An hour later Mom strides in with purpose. "Daniel!" She's carrying three giant pads of paper and an industrial pack of black markers in her arms. She puts everything on the kitchen table and starts sketching Gupta's Grocery right away, her coat still on. If Chain knew about this, I'd be dead for sure.

"So how was work?" I ask, already getting a bad feeling.

"I quit," she says, not looking up, numbers exploding on the page from under her rapidly moving marker. "They accused me of hurting the numbers. I would never hurt the numbers. I just had to hide a few to keep them safe. A battle is coming. The fours and sixes need to be protected."

I move closer and look at her picture. She's drawn flames shooting out of the top of Gupta's Grocery, the smoke mixed with sevens. Fives all around the door. Hollow people haunting the edges of the page, some with swirls and some without.

"What's up with Gupta's?" I ask.

"It's the apex. Very bad."

"Why's it on fire?"

"To burn the badness out."

I pretty much abandon Mom at that point. Go and hide in my room. Dustin's already in his, playing his Nintendo DS. I can hear the bleeps through the door.

I wonder, as I have countless times before, if Mom is capable of doing more than just writing calculations. Would she burn down Gupta's Grocery to close the apex of evil? I remember a sci-fi show a while back. It was about shadows that ate people. This guy kept yelling about counting the shadows and staying out of dark places. In the show, he was right — people were dying all around him, and he was having a tough time keeping his friends safe. If this were TV, Mom would be right. She would actually be saving the world with all her drawings and calculations. But this isn't TV, and she isn't saving anyone. She's just sick.

I think of my homework tucked in my back-pack. Mr. Johnston wants us to write a report exploring the impact of globalization on our lives. I can only think of the impact of my mother on my life right now. I make up a report in my head. Point one, I think, picking up my bass and throwing on the headphones before playing: my mom is men-tally ill. Point two, I think, as I begin to play the bass line from D.O.A.'s "Class War": she doesn't want me or Dustin to be anywhere but home — or school, in Dustin's case — where she knows we're safe. Point three: I'm worried I might start counting one day. Conclusion: I need to escape. I need some normality. It's too early to head down to the Night Owl and see Tracy and her friends, so I put down the bass and call Heather.

After her phone rings a few times, a message clicks on. Of course. She said she was busy to-night. I almost hang up. I'm just going to sound like a dork, but as the message ends I quickly say what's on my mind: "Hey Heather, it's Dan. Do you want to go out for coffee or something after school tomorrow?"

Chapter 15

With Dustin willing to walk himself home today and hang out in his room, and with Mom so deep in her numbers she barely noticed I left for school this morning, I try to put my problems as far out of my mind as possible. Instead, I'm focusing on the task of trying not to screw up my first official date with Heather. Okay, maybe Tim Hortons isn't a huge deal to most people, but in my book it's like taking that first step on the moon. Houston, Dan has landed.

Heather laughs as she talks about her bandmate Maggie, the drummer. She sounds like a real piece of work. She boxes, drums, and drives a big half-ton truck. "So," Heather says, "when we get good, Maggie can drive our equipment to all the gigs."

"That's cool," I say. "I've been on stage once." Then I blush, realizing my blunder. "Oh yeah. You were there for that."

"You were excellent," she says, touching my hand. "I was really happy when I found out we went to the same school."

My face heats up even more and I turn to look at the menu boards, hoping she won't notice. "So," I try to keep the conversation going without sounding completely lame, "what kind of music do you play? Original or covers or…"

"Mostly covers right now," she says. "Motor-head, Metallica, Children of Bodom, that kind of stuff. We were trying to write our own stuff, but nothing's really come out of that."

"I'm working on some lyrics for a song."

Her face lights up. "Can I see?"

"Sure." I shrug like it's no big deal while my brain screams out "*Yes!*" I reach into my backpack and pull out a coil-bound notebook. "It's called 'Psycho Mom.'"

She laughs. "It must be about my mom."

"Really?" I half wish that Heather might be dealing with the same things as me. Leading the same double life.

"She thinks I'm still five." Heather goes on. "I can't do anything without her hovering."

My hope withers and I feel stupid.

"She's always in my face. Always trailing me around." Heather puts on a nasally voice: "Want a cracker? Want a drink? Let me do that for you." She huffs. "I can't even think."

Getting an idea, I start jotting down her words into the notebook under my own, making up the next stanza of the song.

"Hey," she pulls the notebook away from me. "What are you doing?"

"It's good," I say. "Just add a bass line like this ... " I play air bass, bom bom boming the tune to her. In between my vocal bass I start to create a chorus: "*My mom is a psycho.*"

Heather grabs the pen and starts to copy the words.

"*Lost in a world of her own. Loves to play with numbers. Queen of the sudoku zone. Always wants me close. Needs me by her side. I'm about to suffocate. Ready to explode my mind.*"

"Hey this is getting good." Heather smiles.

I take the book back. "It's still rough, but we could have a guitar solo here." I point to a break in the lines.

"Like this?" Heather screeches out an air guitar solo, her arm flying in circles.

"You play guitar?" I ask.

"I just started learning," she says settling back in her seat.

"Let's see." I take her fingers in my hand and touch her soft, pink fingertips. "You have a ways to go."

"Let's see yours." She takes my callous-tipped fingers, rubbing her own over them. Then her hands drift up my arm. My breath catches in my chest. The scent of soft peach soap rises off her skin. She brings her face in close, her warm breath brushing my lips. My heart thuds a thrash metal beat. Then we're kissing, tasting each other's cappuccino and bumping the edge of the table with our ribs.

A few minutes later, panting slightly, Heather asks sheepishly: "So, what are your favourite bands?"

I start to answer, but my words die as Chain walks in the door with his friends, Padma on his arm. "Oh, look," Chain says zeroing in on me. "If it isn't the Nutbar and his Nutbar girlfriend."

"Leave us alone, Chain," I growl.

Heather shoots me a worried glance as Chain's friends circle our table and snicker. Padma looks uncomfortable but says nothing.

"Aren't you supposed to be working?" I ask, sneering.

"I was, until your mom came into the store."

The floor feels like it just became a big black pit under me. I look at Heather, willing her to somehow get away. Not hear what Chain is going to say. Not see my humiliation. "We can discuss this later," I say, half under my breath.

"No." Chain shakes his head. "I think you need to hear this now."

"Chain … " I beg.

"She was dragging your little brother and yelling that our store was making you go crazy." He laughs, doubling over. His friends laugh too. "Even your Mom thinks you're nuts. Isn't that awesome?"

"Shut up," I mutter, trying hard not to lose it. If

I start a fight, I'm going to get beat up and Heather will think I'm useless. If I sit here and do nothing, I'm going to look like a coward and Heather will think I'm useless. Great.

"Want to know something else?" Chain asks in singsong.

"Not really," I say, watching Heather's face grow more and more red.

"My dad called the cops on your mom."

My stomach clenches. "Why?"

"Your mom threatened me. That's how I got the afternoon off."

"Where is she?" My heart is frozen at the thought of Mom in jail and Dustin taken to who knows where.

Chain shrugs. "Probably home. The cops let her off with a warning. They're so dumb."

I have to get to Dustin. I have to reassure my mom. I stand, push through Chain's friends, and get outside. Heather rushes out behind me. Through the window I can see everyone laughing and pointing.

"I gotta..." I say. Hate, fear, anger, disappointment, sadness, and nausea all race around my guts as if it's a bad-vibe mosh pit.

"Go home," Heather says, touching my arm. Her own hand is shaking. "I'll see you at school tomorrow."

"Heather..." I say, wishing life my life was so, so different. "I'm sorry."

Chapter 16

The red welt on my cheek doesn't make me look as tough as I was hoping. I study it in the bathroom mirror, running my fingers over it, wincing at the slight contact. The skin around my eye is starting to go red-blue. Mom has a good arm, I'm just lucky I'm stronger than her.

The numbers changed sometime this afternoon when I was out with Heather. They now all point straight to me, and not in a good way. Evidently, I am in serious danger of becoming permanently tainted. To fix this, Mom decided to beat the bad numbers out of me.

Of course, I made a mad dash for my room. I used all my body weight to hold the door closed while she slammed against it. Finally, after sticking numerous charms all over the outside of my door, Mom left me alone. Dustin cried the entire time but there wasn't much I could do. Not without getting thrashed. At least he's still in her good books.

I grab a washcloth and run cold water over it, holding it to my face as I leave the bathroom. The hallway is silent. I listen at Mom's door, heart thumping a quick beat inside my chest, breath so tight I'm barely getting oxygen. Nothing. I open her door. She's passed out in a nest of papers. Covering every surface are her posters, taped up and filled with calculations and drawings. I think I even see one of me, bad numbers being poured in one side and her pulling them out the other.

"Mom," I hiss. She breathes quietly. "Mom," I call louder. She doesn't stir. I creep in, paper crunching and rustling under my feet. Reaching out, I touch her shoulder. No reaction. She just continues to sleep.

I shut her door and move on to Dustin's room. He's the same way. Passed out on his bed, numbers written all over his arms. I slip in and pull the covers over him. He's completely out, having cried himself to sleep.

Finally I go to my room and grab my jacket, carrying my shoes to the hallway and locking the apartment door behind me. I need out. I need happy faces. I need Tracy.

Chapter 17

"Oh my god, Dan, your eye!" Tracy immediately pulls me out of the Night Owl Café and into the relative quiet of the downtown streets. "You look like you need a hug." She wraps her arms around me, our breath white in the icy air, and we stand that way for a long time — my heart beating against my chest, body shaking, eyes staring at the back of Tracy's jacket.

"So what happened?" she asks as we break apart.

I recount the events leading up to my black eye — from the date, to Chain, to being attacked by my mom. "Once I was sure everyone was asleep, I left," I finish. "I just needed to see you. Get out. But maybe . . ."

"Maybe what?"

"Maybe I shouldn't have gone out. What if my mom wakes up? What if she starts in on Dustin?"

"Dan, you're not Dustin's dad. You're his brother and you deserve a life."

"Yeah, that sounds great. Not selfish at all."

"Living your life isn't selfish. I chose to leave home, do my own thing."

"Well, your life is a little different."

"Everyone's life is different, but we all deserve to be happy, don't we? You don't have to ride this out on your mom's terms."

"What do you mean?"

"Well, even if you stay, you can do things your own way. Like now. You're out here instead of home where your mom wants you," Tracy says with a grin. "It shifts the power from her to you."

"Huh?" I ask, not sure what she's talking about.

"I ran away."

"Yeah ... "

"Now my mom can't brag about her little figure skating star."

I raise an eyebrow. "You figure skate?"

Tracy spins on the tip of her runner. "I won a few meets. Not that Mom ever came. She was too busy with her racquetball instructor and social clubs. But she liked the trophies. It made her feel like a good parent. Now her daughter is on the street, begging and starving," Tracy puts the back of her hand to her forehead like some black and white movie starlet, "and she can't brag. She can't say a word."

"So doing that, running away, makes you have power?" I ask, wondering just how solid this theory is.

"Oh yeah." Tracy nods. "And parents will do anything to get it back. They'll want things to return to normal. But to do that, they have to meet your demands."

"So what are you demanding?"

"For my parents to accept me for exactly who I am, and to hang out with me once in a while as a family."

I chuckle. "A teenager who wants to hang out with her parents? You *are* weird."

"I know, eh?" Tracy grins. "I have a meeting with Mom and Dad tomorrow afternoon."

"Nervous?" I ask, glad to be talking about something other than my problems.

"A little. At least Brian is coming with me."

"Brian?"

"The social worker from that outreach program I hooked up with. Remember?"

"Right." I shuffle my rapidly-numbing feet, my mind slipping back into worry about Dustin alone with Mom. "I should go."

Tracy grabs my hand and tugs me toward the café door. "No way. I have an idea. It's jam night."

"But —" I make a weak attempt to pull away.

"You need fun."

Tracy drags me into the Night Owl and up onto the stage. Once there, she waves to Farmer just as he and his band finish their song. Soon Farmer is talking to Case, the bass player, who he convinces to let me borrow his instrument just as three more guys with guitars jump the stage.

"Everyone know 'Stricken' by Disturbed?" Farmer asks, while Case sits on the side, not looking too pleased with the arrangement.

Everyone does and we start. I latch onto the drummer's rhythm and my brain blanks out. My fingers find the chords and the music takes over. For a moment I'm lost in the pure energy. After that, we slide into "Blitzkrieg Bop" by the Ramones. I don't have a chance to leave, not without wrecking the flow. Then Farmer begins "The System" by The Black Pacific and quickly turns that into "Bridge Burning" by the Foo Fighters. It's awesome. Sweat is pouring down my face and I'm jumping and kicking and thrashing on the bass. The pick I borrowed is long gone and my fingernail is bleeding as it tears. I can feel blisters starting to form, my fingertips not yet calloused enough to prevent such things.

"What next?" Farmer pants, finally out of ideas.

"Does everyone know 'Class War' by D.O.A.?" I ask.

Case comes up on the stage. He looks pissed. "Come on, man," he says, pushing his stringy hair out of his eyes. "You gonna give me a chance?"

My fingers squeeze the neck of his bass. I don't want to let this feeling go. I wish I had my bass. I wish we could both play. "One more song," I beg.

"You've had four."

I frown and point my finger at Farmer and his crew. "You have a whole band. You get to play whenever you want."

"So get a band," he spits back. "It's not too freakin' hard to find people to play with. Come on, it's my bass."

"But..." I'm trying to find a bargaining chip, anything to keep playing, when someone falls down the stairs and into the café. A few people jump up to help, but the person, more clothes than flesh, pushes them away. The smell of mould and urine fills the air as the fabric pile gets to its feet. It's an old woman. She looks confused as she points and shakes. "You. You. Yyyou!" she stutters.

"What about us?" Farmer says into the mic. He laughs at the woman. Everyone laughs. Except me. I stand frozen.

"You!" the woman yelps, stumbling further into the room. "Help!"

"What a loony," Case mutters under his breath. "Someone should just shoot her."

Tracy moves forward. She grabs the woman by the elbow and tries to calm her. "What do you need help with?"

"Help!" the woman yowls again. It sounds like a cat right before it barfs. "I need help. I don't have any help."

"Yeah," Farmer says. "Join the club."

This brings forth more cackles and a few catcalls. I see the owner, Gordon, calling nine-one-one.

"Help!" the woman responds. "Help! I need help!" She points her knobby finger at Tracy, then

Farmer, finally landing on me. "I need help! You! Where are you?"

That's it. I can't take any more. My head is hot then cold, my breath squeezed. I shove the instrument back at Case, snag my coat, dodge past the woman, and run. I have to get home. I have to make sure Dustin's safe. I never should have left.

Chapter 18

My chest is burning by the time I hit my block. My legs are pumping and my jacket flaps against my sides. Every part of my brain is firing the message: Get home. Check on Dustin. Get home. Check on Dustin. So when I see Dustin standing in his SpongeBob pyjamas outside the apartment, arms wrapped tight around his torso, bare feet hopping on the icy concrete, I think I'm seeing an illusion. Something my panicked brain dreamed up.

"Dustin?" I say out loud, still not sure if it's him.

"Dan!" He starts crying and runs to me, wrapping his arms around my waist. His skin feels so cold.

"What are you doing out here?"

Dustin punches me and jumps away. "You lied."

"Huh?" I'm still trying to figure out why my

brother is outside in his pyjamas at one-thirty in the morning.

"You said you didn't go out."

"You followed me?" I ask, taking out my key and unlocking the door to let us both into the lobby.

"No!" His face twists in frustration. "Mom woke up."

My knees drop out from under me. I grab his shoulders. "Oh, Dustin. I am so, so sorry."

He twists away and starts pacing, hands shaking. "I got up because I had a bad dream. So I went to your room. Except you weren't there." He glares. "I was going to go back to bed, but I was hungry. So I went to the kitchen and tried to get a plate down for toast. But I dropped the plate and it smashed." Dustin's eyes go big. He stands, reliving the experience. "The noise woke up Mom. She thought I was attacking her. She pushed me down on the floor and tried to cut me with a piece of the plate."

I run my eyes over every part of my little brother. No blood. No visible cuts. "Did she?"

"No. I got away and ran out of the apartment. I thought you might be checking the mail, so I came downstairs. But you weren't."

Knees still jelly, I push myself to a stand. "Why did you go outside?"

"I wanted to see if you were, you know, coming back from a walk or something. The door locked behind me and I couldn't get back in."

"How long were you out there?"

"I don't know. It was really cold."

"Come on," I say, leading him over to the elevator and pushing the button. "Let's go home."

Dustin shakes his head and steps back. "Not if she's still awake."

I take his trembling hand in mine. "We can listen at the door."

Back on the second floor, we both listen with our ears pressed to the door. I don't hear anything — no chanting or paper being torn. Quietly, I turn the handle. It's locked. Mom locked Dustin out. An overwhelming feeling of frustration and anger rushes through me. Why is she so selfish? What the hell could a nine-year-old do to a full-grown woman?

I almost take Dustin and turn around, head back to the Night Owl. Run away like Tracy. Except Dustin has no shoes or coat and I think he's had enough trauma for one night. I pull out my key.

Inside, the apartment is dark. I can see the broken plate on the floor. Everything else is as it was when I left. Mom must have gone back to bed. With Dustin still out in the hallway, I creep to her room and listen. Nothing. I twist the knob and look inside. She's back in her nest of papers, breathing lightly.

I think, briefly, of what would happen if I were to cut her like she tried to do to Dustin. If I took a piece of that plate, or better yet, a knife, and sliced her throat. Would anyone care? Would anyone miss her? Would I miss her?

I clench my fists against these crazy thoughts. I don't want to be like her. I don't want to be a lunatic. Carefully, I pull the door shut and get Dustin. It takes a few minutes before he's willing to come back in. Together we silently sweep up the plate and creep to my room. He curls into bed beside me, his body still trembling even though he's warm now.

"Dan?" he asks.

"Yeah?"

"I wish Mom wouldn't talk to numbers."

"So do I."

"I wish she liked us better than them."

"I'm not sure it works that way."

Dustin lays silently, our breath sounding like a quiet song. "Mom loved me when we went to Hawaii, right?"

"Mom still loves you," I say, but I'm not entirely sure anymore.

"Then why would she think I would hurt her?"

I take a deep breath and let it out slowly. "She was probably still dreaming."

"It was scary."

I hug him close and think of what Tracy said about not having to live by my mom's terms. About shifting some of the power to us. I doubt it would work the way she thinks it will, but after what Dustin and I have been through tonight, I'm willing to give anything a try.

"Dustin?"

"Yeah?"

"Tomorrow, things are going to change. We're going to start having fun."

Chapter 19

By morning the bruise on my cheek and around eye has gone from red-blue to purple-green. And I still don't look tough. I have a shower, hoping to stop the spinning in my stomach. When I return to the bedroom, Dustin is finally sitting up. He's still worn out from last night. "Come on kid, isn't there something you want to do at school today?"

He shakes his head, still too sleepy to be verbal.

"I guess you don't want to pick a pumpkin for Halloween."

"Huh?" his face is blank until he remembers that his class is going to Butterfield Acres to get Halloween decorations for the school.

I saw the trip written in blocky printing on the kitchen calendar. Dustin only does that when it's something he's excited about, like special Sponge-Bob episodes or field trips. But even though he's raring to go, he won't let me out of his sight. He insists I come to his room and stay while he dresses. Watch him in the bathroom while he brushes his teeth. We both take granola bars outside with us, partly because we're starting to run late and partly because Dustin is worried Mom will wake up before we're out the door.

I have to admit, I am too.

I drop Dustin off at school with a quiet warning not to mention last night to anyone. My thoughts turn again to Grandma and Aunt Clara. We've been out of contact with them for so long they might not even remember us. And if they do, they might want nothing to do with us. Not if it means dealing with Mom again.

My morning ends up going surprisingly well. I catch my bus and get to school with enough time to go to my locker before my first class. The classroom is teacher-free when I slink in and grab my usual desk near the back. Heather slides into the desk next to me.

"What happened to you?" she asks, reaching up to touch my cheek. I shiver inside. "Did Chain do this?"

I look around. Chain isn't here yet. "No."

"Who then?"

I shrug.

"Come on, you didn't do it to yourself," she says.

"Maybe I did," I say, then change the subject. "Are you still jamming after school?"

Heather beams. "Absolutely. Can you still make it?"

"Oh yeah. I am so there."

"I hope you're bringing your brother. I told Tyler he would have someone to play video games with. He's bummed because his best friend is gone for the weekend."

"Yeah, we'll both be there. I just have to pick up my bass and amp first."

"Don't worry about the amp," she says. "I have a spare. I'll give you my address."

Heather writes on a page of loose leaf and tears it out of her binder just as Chain swaggers in. "Hey Nutbar, you're here! I thought you were still running. I guess you're not too chicken to show your face." He notices my black eye and grimaces. "And what an ugly face it is, too. Looks like you pissed someone else off. Ready for your beating?" He slams his fist into my already-bruised shoulder, sending lightning bolts through my vision.

I'm halfway out of my desk and ready to pound Chain when Mr. Johnston walks in. Heather grabs the waistband of my jeans and pulls me back into my seat while Chain scurries to sit in the desk next to Padma. She turns her head, picks up her books, and moves to a spot on the far side of the room. Mr. Johnston starts calling attendance.

Chapter 20

Back at the apartment, Dustin decides to wait in the hallway. He's still jittery from last night. Not to mention he got into another fight at school and has a bit of a bruise on his cheek. Mom's not going to like that, and he knows it. Serves him right, though. He really needs to settle down.

Mom's at the kitchen table when I walk in. I'm still carrying my backpack. It's kind of stupid, but I feel so happy about seeing Heather in less than an hour that nothing Mom says or does can mess that up. That and, as of last night, I really don't care about her drama anymore. I have my own things to do.

"You!" She jumps up and grabs at my shirt.

I leap back, dodging her. "What?"

"You went to school!" Her eyes dart around my head, like she can't focus on anything.

"Yeah," I answer, moving past her to my room.

She follows, slapping the walls with her palms. "They're going to hurt you."

I dump my backpack on my bed and grab my bass, laying it in its soft-shell carrying case and zipping up the side. Mom looms in the doorway, blocking my exit.

"What are you doing?" she demands.

"Going out."

"No you're not!" Her face is red and her eyes are narrowed. She strikes me as a life-sized Malibu Barbie — the super-angry version.

"Yes." I stand and sling the bass over my shoulder. "I am."

I go to push past her but she grabs my wrist. Heart pounding, breath tight, I yank my hand out of her grip and continue down the hall to the living room.

"Where's Dustin?" she asks.

I hesitate. If I tell her, she'll snatch him up and I'll never get out of here. If I don't, she'll freak. "He's coming with me."

"I don't even know where you're going." She's almost crying.

"Just to jam."

"But where?" She grabs onto my bass and yanks, wrenching my shoulder under the strap. "Where are you going?"

"To a friend's house."

"Friends. From that school, right?"

"Yeah, I met her at school." I lunge forward with my whole body and rip free from Mom's fingers, then spin around to face her, backing away slowly. "We'll be back for dinner. You can make something nice and we can all hang out together."

"Why can't you see, Daniel?" she pleads. "Why can't you see what they're doing to you?"

I twist the doorknob, pull the door open behind me. My legs feel like Jell-O and I'm shaking pretty bad. So much for adrenalin — all it does is make me want to puke. Slipping out and slamming the door, I grab Dustin by the hand and run down the hallway. Dustin looks like he's about to throw up too. His face is white and his eyes are huge. I practically throw him into the emergency stairwell. There is no way I'm waiting for an elevator with Mom on my tail.

"I won't let you taint Dustin!" I hear Mom call. "I won't let you have him!"

It's not until we're three blocks away that we stop running. Dustin and I make eye contact while bending over to catch our breath. We both know this isn't the end of it. There will be more when we get back home. But for now, Dustin smiles at me and I smile back. We're in this together.

We hop a bus to Heather's house. It's a nice place, just over the Elbow River from downtown. She lives in a little house with a big backyard and a heated garage. The garage is where the equipment's set up. Lanky, black-haired Sebastian is throwing out power chords on his guitar and Maggie is tightening her drum kit. She's a tough-looking girl with raspberry-coloured hair and a face full of freckles. She looks like she could beat Chain Gupta in a fight. Her face lights up when she sees me. "You made it!"

I shrug. "Here I am."

Heather comes back from finding her little brother, Tyler. Tyler has the same blond hair as his sister, only his is messy and wild. He looks resentfully at us. I know exactly what he's thinking and guilt comes flooding through me once more. He doesn't want to be forced to play with a kid he's never met. Dustin looks upset too. Like escaping Mom wasn't enough excitement for one day.

"Hi Tyler," I say, trying to break the ice. "This is Dustin."

Tyler says nothing, just stares at us. Dustin grabs the corner of my jacket.

"So, umm…" I try to find some common ground. "Do you like SpongeBob?"

Tyler puts his hands on his hips and sticks his chest out. "I just got *SpongeBob's Truth or Square* for the Wii."

"Can two people play that?" Heather asks.

"Duh," Tyler answers. In a barely hushed whisper, he says to Dustin, "Sisters."

Dustin says nothing, but I can see he's interested. His fear of this new place is starting to fade. As long as his buddy SpongeBob is here, what could go wrong?

"Well?" Heather says, nudging Tyler.

"What?" he snaps at her.

"Ask Dustin if he wants to play."

Tyler is starting to look a little red in the ears. "Do you play Wii?"

Dustin nods. It's his favourite thing at after-school care — when he isn't banned from it for fighting.

"Then come on. But I get to be Sandy. She has some sweet martial arts moves."

Dustin lets go of my jacket and follows Tyler. Heather watches them cross the yard. Her mom comes out of the house and tells the boys something before heading over to the garage. She's carrying a plate of apple slices and some crackers. "A snack for the future Top of the Pops," she says, entering.

Sebastian and Maggie groan. "Mom," Heather whines, "metal bands aren't pop."

Heather's mom laughs, flicking her blond hair back just the way Heather does. Her blue eyes are a little deeper than her daughter's but shining with the same mischief. "Well, just remember who brought you snacks when you make it big."

"Will do," Sebastian says, giving her a two-finger salute.

Heather's mom stands staring at me. I squirm under the attention. "Well," she finally says to her daughter. "Aren't you going to introduce us?"

Heather blushes. "Oh, sorry. This is Dan, Dustin's brother. He plays the bass."

"And if he's good enough, we'll let him join," Maggie says, chewing on an apple slice.

"I'm Karen." Heather's mom sticks out her hand and I shake it. It's starting to creep me out, the way she's looking at me. "Dan and Dustin," she says thoughtfully. "I believe I've met your mother."

"Oh yeah?" I ask, getting a bad feeling.

"She came to the first School Council meeting. Made quite a stir."

I swallow.

"She said something about changing the name of the school and firing the principal. She was very intense about it." She looks at me closely, her gaze settling on my bruised eye.

My face turns eight shades of red. Heather has probably heard all about the School Council meeting. She's probably known all along that my mom is schizo. So why does she want me here? Because I'm some sort of oddity? Or is it just for my bass? There's no way she could really like me. Not if she knows.

"You boys look like you've been fighting," Heather's mom continues. "You must like rough-housing as much as my Tyler. Did Dustin get his bruise from you?"

It must look bad — me with a black eye and Dustin with a bruised cheek. I'm starting to wish I hadn't come. "Dustin got into a fight at school," I explain, telling the truth for once. "Some kid was bugging him."

"Oh," Heather's mom says, obviously unsure whether to believe me. "Okay. Well, if you or your brother need someone to talk to or —"

It's then that I notice Heather is looking as pink as I feel. "Yeah, yeah," she says, physically pushing her mother out the garage door. "He knows. Now go. We have to practice." Heather shrugs and smiles as her mother finally takes the path across the yard to the house. "Sorry about that. I told you ... psycho mom."

"That's not psycho," Sebastian says. "My mom practically needs an itinerary before she lets me leave the house."

"No, no, guys." Maggie holds up her hands. "My mom wins the psycho award. At my boxing matches she gets so into it I'm afraid she's going to start hitting the guy next to her."

"I guess having a psycho mom is pretty common," I shrug.

Maggie thumps her drums. "Let's play."

"What song first?" Heather asks. She turns to me. "What do you know?"

"I know a lot of D.O.A. stuff," I say, pointing to my D.O.A. shirt.

"Never heard of them," Sebastian says, blasting out a screaming lead. "How about Children of Bodom?"

"Sure," I say, unzipping my case and plugging my bass into the free amp.

"Let's do it!" Maggie screams, counting us in.

The music flows and Heather's voice goes instantly from sweet to heavy metal queen. In moments I'm lost in the music, slamming down one song after another and learning a few in between. By five thirty, I'm soaked with sweat and happy.

Maggie throws down a drum solo and then suggests one more song before she has to go. "How about 'Blood on Your Hands' by Arch Enemy?"

Heather pumps her fist in the air. "My favourite song. You know that one, Dan?"

I think about how fast that bass line is and inwardly cringe. I've played it before, but it's always tangled my fingers. "Sure," I reply, hoping that I don't mess up.

It goes well — only a few dropped notes. Maggie lays a steady beat for me to follow and I keep on track. After everyone has left, Heather wraps her arm around my waist and kisses me on the cheek. "I'm glad you came, Dan," she says.

"Me too," I reply, taking her in my arms and giving her a real kiss. All the embarrassment and tension caused by Chain and his gang the day before vanishes. Before I leave for home, I promise Heather I'll jam again tomorrow and bring Dustin too, not even caring about Mom or what she thinks.

The entire bus ride home, Dustin looks just as happy as I feel. He can't shut up about Tyler — his new best friend — the excellent SpongeBob game, or the fact that he wants a Wii for Christmas. While I half listen to him describing the cool moves he performed in *Super Smash Bros. Brawl*, I dream of Heather. The way she whipped her hair around, and how she vocally changed from sweet angel to ravaged demon then back again as each song finished. The way she felt in my arms. I have to hold back a chuckle when I think of her doing Motorhead's "Ace of Spades" with the mic way up above her just like Lemmy.

Dustin finally quiets down when we transfer buses. He gazes silently out the window, looking relaxed. I realize it's been forever since he's played with another kid outside of after-school care. It seems like Tracy's idea to take control of our lives was a good plan after all. Dustin gets to act like a normal nine-year-old and I get to see Heather — and play music. It's so perfect.

Chapter 21

Walking home from the bus stop, I spot Chain coming down the street. He probably saw me from Gupta's Grocery. I cringe. What a way to mess up this awesome afternoon. But he's smiling. Maybe he's happy because he gets to punch the crap out of me with no teachers to stop him.

"Nutbar!" Chain calls, raising his arm.

"Chain," I reply, without enthusiasm. "What's up?"

"You're off the hook," he states.

"Oh yeah?" I ask.

Chain comes to a stop in front of us and lays his hand on my shoulder in a brotherly way. Dustin scowls at him. "Guess who's back behind the counter?" he asks.

"Your grandma?"

"Yup." Chain grins. "Grandma's finally back. That means no more working till midnight for me and," he punches my shoulder lightly, "no more beatings for you. Well, at least not for that."

"Good to hear," I say, a little unsure about the lingering threat. "Is she working tonight?"

"Has been for a few hours. I was just stocking. Now all I have to do is help her close the store and walk her upstairs. That gives me all sorts of time with Padma."

I remember the classroom incident this morning. "Is she still talking to you?"

He winks and nudges me. "She's just playing hard to get." He continues down the sidewalk, calling out behind him, "Later, Nutbar."

Dustin looks up at me, squinting. "That was weird," he says.

"Definitely," I agree.

"At least you won't get into fights at school anymore," he says, as we continue walking again.

"No, just you."

Dustin reaches up and touches his bruised cheek. "It's not my fault all the kids say I have a crazy mom."

I rub his head. "You could just ignore them."

Dustin pulls away, his eyes flashing. "Never!"

The caretaker greets us in the lobby of our apartment building reeking of overcooked cabbage and possibly boiled goat. He glares at me in that Russian spy way of his and clicks his tongue. "So," he says, "back at last."

I raise an eyebrow. "Huh?"

"Your mother . . ."

My heart freezes mid-beat.

"She was down here, frantic," he continues. "Said you'd run away."

A cold wave hits me so bluntly I can barely get the words out. "Where is she now?"

"I took her back to her apartment. Said I'd send you up when you came back. But... I'm not so sure."

Dustin looks at him bewildered. "Not sure about what?"

The caretaker lays a thick-knuckled hand on Dustin's head, his eyes kind. "I think, maybe, you should go away. Your mother... there's something wrong up here." He taps his temple with a gnarled finger. "Getting worse, no?"

"She's just..." I start to lie, but can't continue — don't want to continue. Instead I turn and push the elevator button.

"As you like." The caretaker shrugs, going back to his apartment. I catch him casting an uneasy glance over one shoulder before he closes the door. The elevator dings and we get in.

On the second floor, outside the apartment door, I hear Mom thumping around. The sound of paper being torn from a pad. Dustin looks panicked.

"It's going to be okay," I whisper. "I won't let anything happen to you."

I push the door open. Mom is bent over, drawing a large picture of Gupta's Grocery, her hand moving quickly. Chaotic drawings cover everything from the TV to the couch. They line the floor, dangle like flags from the ceiling. It's a maze of paper. There are no more grey pencil smudges on these pages. Thick black lines outline pictures of buildings, numbers, hollow people, and flames. The air is ripe with off-gassing markers. I could get high just by breathing.

"Hey Mom," I say, pretending everything is normal. Pretending her drama no longer affects me. "What did you make for dinner?"

"You're back!" Mom says, a brief smile filling her tense face. She rushes at Dustin, pulling him into her arms, and goes over him methodically, checking every inch. "What have you done to him?" She wrenches his head, turning Dustin's purplish, bruised cheek toward me.

My stomach tenses. "He got into a fight at school," I explain.

"Liar," she snaps. "Dustin doesn't fight. Do you, baby?"

Dustin's looking frantic, his eyes darting from me to Mom and back again. I'm not feeling much calmer.

"It's just a little bruise," I say. "He's fine."

"I'll decide if he's fine!" Mom yells. She turns her attention back to Dustin. "Did your mean big brother hit you? Let me get you some ice."

Still gripping Dustin's arm, she pulls him to the kitchen and opens the freezer, taking out a small ice pack and putting it directly on Dustin's cheek.

He tries to pull away. "That's too cold."

"Don't be silly. It's the best thing," Mom soothes, pressing harder.

"Ow!" Dustin cries. "Stop it." He pulls hard and frees himself from Mom's grip, then runs to me.

"What's wrong with you?" Mom says, her face contorting with frustration. "I'm trying to help."

"What's wrong with you?" I demand. "Ice packs need to be wrapped in a cloth."

"Oh, you think you know everything!" Mom growls. "Take it then." She fast-balls the ice pack, hitting me in the chest, then turns back to her work, muttering under her breath. I pick it up off the floor and hand it to Dustin. "Go get a cloth from the bathroom," I tell him.

The fumes from Mom's industrial-style markers are starting to make me feel dizzy. I walk to the window and pull it open, tearing a sheet of paper in the process. Mom runs over, sliding on paper that covers the floor, and grabs the torn sheet. She pushes the two halves of the paper into my face, shaking them. "You wreck everything!"

Rushing to the kitchen, she rifles through the junk drawer with one hand while holding the torn paper up in the other. Finally, half the drawer emptied onto the floor, she pulls out a roll of electrical tape, black like the marker. She waves it at me like it's a charm to ward off evil and goes to the table to repair the paper. I head to my room, determined not to play along with her fantasies. Dustin is there, flopped onto my bed.

"Something wrong with your room?" I snarl. I'm tired and hungry and Mom didn't make anything for supper.

Dustin puts his head in his hands and curls up into a ball.

"Sorry, buddy," I mumble, guilt overwhelming me again. I realize he probably feels the same way I do.

"I want to go back to Tyler's house," he says thickly.

I swing my bass off my shoulders and stand it beside my amp, then sit next to him. "Me too."

"Why ... " He's sobbing too hard to speak properly. "Why does she have to be like this? Tyler's mom had cookies and fruit. Why does ours have numbers and paper?"

I almost laugh. What he's saying isn't funny, but the image of Mom looking like a fifties housewife, carrying a snack plate filled with pads of paper and magnetic numbers, pops into my head. "I don't know, kid." I give him a hug and he calms down. "Are you hungry?"

He shrugs.

"Well, I am," I say, heading back out the door. "I'll make some food."

"Okay, but hurry."

In the living room, Mom greets me with a glare. "What are you two doing in there?"

"Nothing," I say, moving past her and opening the fridge. It's pretty sparse. I close the door and look in the cupboard. There's spaghetti and a can of sauce. That's good enough. I begin filling a pot with hot water in the sink. Our apartment has intensely hot water. Other tenants complain, but I like it. It makes cooking so much quicker.

Mom stands way too close behind me. She reaches around my body and grabs the pot, dumping the water into the sink. Half of it sloshes up and onto the floor, making my socks, the dropped junk-drawer stuff, and sheets of random paper wet. I dance, trying to cool down my burning toes. "Ow! Mom!"

"I know what you're doing," she hisses in my ear.

My stomach rumbles. Jamming took a lot of energy and I'm starving. I snatch back the pot and begin filling it once more.

She grabs at it again and I pull it away, spilling some of the water down my shirt. My stomach stings. "Arrgh! What is your problem?" I yell.

"You can't fool me, you're infected by sevens."

I turn the burner on high, put on the pot, then start to open the can of sauce, getting it ready.

She eyes me severely, muttering, "Seven, seven, seven." Then she marches to the table and grabs her marker. Returning, she starts to write on the back of my shirt. I arch, pushing her away and knocking my elbow against the burner. The pain ignites my rage.

"Crap! Mom, cut it out! Stop being so schizo!"

"You're a betrayer!" She screams, coming at me again, marker extended. "I have to neutralize you."

"I don't care about your stupid numbers anymore!" I dodge and feel the marker drag across my cheek. Leaping past her into the living room, I spit in my palm and wipe frantically at the mark. I don't want to look like a freak when I see Heather again.

Mom follows me, marker extended. "You must be dealt with."

For the first time since we arrived home, I see my mom. Really see her. Her dirty-blond hair streaked with black marker, her eyes sunken and dark, her face gaunt, nails chipped and chewed. And she's coming at me like I'm the one who's the monster.

Boiling water might not be my brightest idea.

Mom aims the marker at my chest. I twist and jump behind the couch. "Stop it!" I'm wearing my white D.O.A., Will Rise Again, shirt. Right now, it's my favourite piece of clothing. After all, Heather touched it. I won't let Mom wreck it.

"You need to be cleansed."

"Marker is definitely not going to cleanse me," I tell her.

Mom stops and shakes her head, a hint of a smile appearing on her lips. "The marker doesn't cleanse, Daniel, the good numbers do. They'll help remove the poison that school has put in you."

The water in the kitchen begins to hiss, getting close to a boil. I dodge past her and dump the noodles in. She advances once more.

"Numbers are just numbers," I say, leaping away from the pot of blisteringly hot water and back out to the living room. I don't want to lead her to a weapon. Marker is bad enough.

"You're wrong! How can you not see?" She stops to examine a paper on the wall, her pen dropping to her side, fingers tracing the calculations. "Oh, I understand." She starts writing on the sheet. Alphabet codes, dates, hollow people, and arrows. Thank you, short attention span.

Back in the kitchen, I start humming Motorhead's "Ace of Spades" under my breath, remembering Heather's performance in the garage. Man is she awesome. I think about her mom's offer of help. Would she understand what I'm going through, or would she ban me from seeing Heather ever again? I mean, mental illness isn't just something you announce. People think it rubs off.

I hunt for a strainer in the bottom cupboard, and I'm so caught up in my thoughts that I don't realize Mom has stopped writing until she moves between me and the stove.

"Daniel, it's not your fault," she says slowly, her eyes focused on the boiling water.

"That's good to hear."

She grabs the handle of the pot, not moving it. Inside, bubbles jump and snap, white noodles dancing just under the water's surface. "Your dad had the wrong name."

"Oh yeah?" I try to keep her calm.

"He had bad numbers deep inside him."

"That sucks."

"That's why you've become so evil."

I shake my head. This is surreal. I feel like I'm in a really bad movie, full of rubber monsters and swords made of tin. "Mom," I step forward, reaching for the spaghetti pot, trying to figure out how to get it away from her without spilling the boiling water all over myself. "I'm fine. I love you." At this point I'm not sure if I'm lying or not.

I put my hand over hers. Both our fingers cover the handle.

"I know you think that," she says. "But this is deeper." She yanks the pot. The water sloshes, burning both our hands. She yelps. I swear. The pot slams back onto the stove, burner hissing, smoke rising from the spilled noodles. She grabs for it again. I throw the strainer at her head, beat her to the pot, and toss the whole thing in the sink. Noodles slither down the drain.

I turn on the tap and run cold water over my lobster-coloured hand, while trying to scoop the remaining noodles back into the pot with the other. Exhaustion floods through me. I watch Mom wrap paper around her wound, tape it down, and write numbers on it.

"That's not going to help," I tell her. "You need cold water or ice." I run some water on a cloth and hold it out toward her.

"Don't touch me," she growls, slumping in a chair and starting to draw again, her paper glove crinkling.

Slamming the cloth on the counter, I return to rescuing supper. The noodles are still a bit crunchy and only half of them make it back into the pot. I finish opening the can of sauce and pour it over the noodles, then take the whole pot and two forks to my room. Mom doesn't even look up as I pass.

Chapter 22

Back in my room, I grab Dustin's lukewarm ice pack and put it on my stinging hand. The relief is amazing.

"What happened?" Dustin asks, picking up a fork and eating out of the pot.

"A tug of war with the spaghetti," I tell him.

He looks at me like I'm nuts. I switch the ice pack to my elbow where it grazed the burner. Right away, my hand starts screaming again.

"I'm thirsty," he says.

I'm not going back out there. "Get a drink from the bathroom," I tell him.

"But I don't want water," he whines.

I glare.

"Okay, okay," he says, getting up. "You don't have to get so mad."

It seems like forever before he's done eating and I've got him tucked into bed in my room. I just need some quiet.

Staring out the window, I look along the sky-line, all orange and black. I can't see any stars. Not with the glare of the city. I think of what life would be like if I just took Dustin and ran. Could we make it? And what would happen to Mom? Would she finally go off the deep end? I sigh and lay my forehead against the frosty glass. Too many problems. That's all my life is, too many problems.

My blistered hand starts throbbing again. The cloth I wrapped it in after dinner is too warm now. I open my bedroom door and cross the hall to the bathroom. Mom is asleep, or at least there's no noise coming out of her room. After running cold water over my skin and wetting the cloth once more, I make a quick detour to the living room for the white pages and the phone before hiding back in my room.

In the glow of my desk lamp, I open the phone book to a random page and run my finger down the micro-print. I know what I'm looking for. Grand-ma. Has her number changed? I open Mom's old address book. Her writing is cramped and spidery. But it doesn't give a name. Just Grandma/Mom. I don't think I ever knew what Grandma's real name was.

I start to dial the number but chicken out half-way through and close the address book. I check the red welt on my elbow and the blisters on my hand, and feel the bruise on my cheek and eye. Grandma wouldn't want to get involved with this.

No one would. I just wish I knew what to do.

Bored and jumpy, I flip through the phone book again, coming across a bright yellow page with emergency numbers. My life feels like an emergency, but I think the people manning 911 probably wouldn't agree. After that page are long-distance area codes for places like New Jersey, Texas, and Spain. A bright pink section follows. I always figured the pink part was girl's stuff but what I see makes me shudder. A box with the title, "Frequently Called Numbers." Two of them are for mental health. My mom needs to talk to these people. I wonder how I can get her to call.

I think about calling them myself. Maybe asking if they could come over and calm Mom down. Give her some pills. Then I look at my hand. No — they would just take her away. You can't burn your kids and stay in the house with them afterward. I sigh. It seems an impossible situation.

It's only ten o'clock. Not too late at night. I wonder if Heather's mom would really help. I start to call, but hang up after punching the first two digits. Telling Heather, asking her mom — it's like admitting that I have a problem. And I don't — my mom does. Still, I feel like I'm going to be blamed.

I picture the Night Owl all the way downtown. It seems like the other side of the world. I wish I could go, but Dustin's snuffling snores remind me I can't. Yet Tracy is really the only one I can talk to. I wish she were here.

In the end, I decide to try to sleep. To prepare, I put a monster band-aid for skinned knees over the burn on my elbow and wrap my hand in a clean, damp t-shirt. It's still throbbing, but the pain is manageable. The tick of a stone hitting the window makes me jump.

I get up to look and see Tracy outside in the parking lot. My heart skips. It's like she read my mind. I grin and wave — she doesn't smile back. In fact, it looks like she's crying. Then I remember: today was the meeting with her parents. I wave again and point down, then I grab my jacket and gingerly slip my hand through the armhole. Just going to the parking lot should be all right. It's not like I'll be that far away.

Chapter 23

Dustin stirs and looks up as I'm sliding out of the room.

"Where are you going?" he asks, his sleepy eyes suddenly growing wide.

"Just to the parking lot for a sec."

"But..." Dustin starts to whimper. "But what if Mom comes in?"

I poke my head out the bedroom door. The apartment is still quiet. No sound from anywhere. "She's asleep."

"But what if —" Dustin asks, his face pale.

"If Mom wakes up, shout down to me and I'll be right up."

He looks unconvinced. "How? It's too cold to leave the window open."

I go to my bedroom window, my breath fogging up the glass. Tracy has her back turned and is rubbing her gloved hands together. I grip the edge and tug. The window cracks open, letting in a blast of cold air and car exhaust. "See?" I say, showing Dustin. "It's not that hard to open. Just slide and yell, and I'll be right up, okay?"

He slowly nods and I close the window, tie up my shoes and check for my keys. Before leaving, I push his head playfully onto the pillow. "Don't worry. I'll be, like, five minutes. Okay?"

"Okay."

"Now close your eyes."

Dustin snuggles down once more and feigns sleep. It's good enough for me. I creep down our hall, away from Mom's room and out of the apartment.

Frost covers the parking lot like a sparkling blanket, making the cars look disco and the ground slippery. Tracy stands shivering near a blue pickup truck, her eyes red and puffy. "I just came to say goodbye." She reaches out to touch my bandaged hand and raises an eyebrow. "What happened to you?"

"Forget me," I respond. "What happened to you? Didn't the power-shifting thing work on your parents?"

She shakes her head, breaking into sobs and wrapping her arms tight around her body as if trying to hold her trembling in. "They're such jerks!" she rants, her eyes blazing. "I'm their only child," she drops her head and mutters, "and they hate me."

"How could they hate you?" I ask, taking her

gloved hand in my good one, our breath coming out in puffs. "You're wonderful."

"My mom wouldn't even look at me. And my dad ... " Tracy covers her face with her hands, before wiping her nose and eyes on the back of her sleeve. "My dad said if I wanted to come back to live with them, I could never see my friends again. Not ever. And I'd be grounded for a year. He said if I couldn't agree to his rules, I may as well live somewhere else." She sniffs and crosses her arms.

"What'd your mom say?" I ask. I think I hear a clink from above and look up, cocking my ear to the sound.

"I don't know. I'd had enough by then. I just left. I can't wait to get to Vancouver! Anywhere is better than here."

"So you've talked to your aunt?" I ask. "She's going to take you in?"

Tracy shakes her head. "I forgot to get her number from my dad. Not that he'd give it to me anyway."

"But ... Tracy, how are you —"

"I'm going to hitch down and figure things out when I get there. I might not even want to live with her. Just because Dad doesn't like her doesn't mean she's nice. Maybe I'll get a job and get my own place. Have a bit of freedom and fun." She grabs me and pulls me close. "You should come with me," Tracy says. "We could have fun together. We could be like boyfriend and girlfriend."

I get the sense Tracy is oversimplifying things

again. The two of us going to Vancouver wouldn't make things any safer or easier. Besides, I have my own problems. I glance up at the window once more. No sound. No movement. Looking back at Tracy, I say, "You don't want me. I'm too easy."

"You're easy?"

"I already like you. You want your parents. It's them you have to convince. You need to show them what an awesome person you are. Show them what I already know."

"I can't."

"You bailed. You ran before you told them how you feel."

"But they won't listen."

"How do you know?"

"I know."

"Tracy, you're so good at fixing everyone else's problems. You need to fix your own now. Talk to your dad. Tell your mom that you need her. Maybe they don't know. Maybe they assume what they did was enough. Anyway," I let go and nudge her with my elbow, giving her a wink, "they're parents, not psychics. They can't read your mind."

"Yeah, you're right, I guess." She looks at me sternly. "But I'll only talk to them to get the phone number." Tracy sighs. "Are you sure you don't want to come to Vancouver with me?"

I shake my head.

"Come on. Just as friends? It would be a party ... "

"I can't," I murmur, I hear a tapping again and

look up at my bedroom window. I still don't see a face or hand, but something feels wrong. "My mom..."

"She's been acting crazy?"

"*Er*." I correct. "She's been acting craz*ier*."

"Oh." Tracy looks up. "You think she's in your room?"

I study my window. I can't see anything, and the noise has stopped, but there's a bad feeling crawling into my gut. "Dustin's in my room. He's worried Mom's going to do something to him."

"Would she?"

I think of the broken plate and feel my breath catch. "Maybe."

She points to my wrapped hand. "Did she do that to you?"

I say nothing.

"Well," Tracy grabs my good hand, "let's get up there and check on the kid."

"Tracy, I don't . . ." I start, but she's already at the back door to the building. I go over and unlock it, catching the smell of fabric softener from the laundry room. "I don't think you should come," I say, turning to block her way. "Things might be..."

Tracy puts one hand on her hip and the other on my shoulder. "You know you need my help, Dan." She shoves me inside. "Now march."

Chapter 24

At the apartment, I'm afraid to open the door. I know I've told Tracy everything, but that's different from seeing it. My blood pressure rises. The pounding of my heartbeat slams against my eardrums. I feel faint. I might hurl. I'm not a huge fan of anxiety.

"What's the holdup?" Tracy asks, watching me with the key in the lock, my hand not turning it.

The holdup is I don't want her to think of me as a freak. What if, once I open the door, she thinks I'm crazy too?

Tracy puts her hand over mine and turns the key. She twists the doorknob and lets us both in. "Oh, wow," she murmurs.

I cringe, seeing the apartment through her eyes. It looks like a primitive cave with hieroglyphs covering every surface. Or Evil Christmas come early, the place all wrapped up. If it weren't me, my place, my family — I'd be running. This just looks so wrong.

"Dan..." Tracy whispers.

"Yeah," I reply, copying her tone.

"Grab your brother, you shouldn't be here." She looks scared. "We can call Brian. He can help, I know he can."

I know what Tracy says is true, my brother and me — we should leave. But part of me still feels guilty at the thought of leaving Mom to face her illness alone. It's not her fault she has schizophrenia. But the disease always seems to take priority over us, and honestly, I'm so tired of living like this.

"I'll get Dustin." I head through the dining room and down the hall. The house is silent. Opening my bedroom door, I immediately trip over Dustin's stuffed dog. Picking it up, I flick on the desk lamp and stare at the bed, trying to make out Dustin's body in the jumble of multi-coloured crazy quilts. The pattern isn't making sense. Striding over, I pat the covers, then pull them back. The bed is empty.

My throat closes. I race across the hall to the bathroom. Maybe he's taking a leak. Nothing. Then Dustin's room. His bed is empty too. That leaves only one more place. Mom probably came in, got Dustin, and took him to her room. She probably thought I was going to kidnap him or something. Slowly I open her bedroom door.

Under the room's white light, the cave of

papers Mom's room has become hits me like a punch to the chest. It's like a monument to her illness, getting worse and worse. But as frightening as that is, there is one thing more frightening. No one is here. The room is empty.

I yell and yell and yell until I'm collapsing from lack of breath and my heart is thudding like it's about to break bones. Where are they? Why did they leave? Why did I leave? I promised ... What if she ... I wish ...

Mr. Jones starts banging on the wall. "Shut up!" He bellows from his apartment. "I'll call the cops."

"That's not a bad idea," Tracy says. She's found me.

"No!" I shake off the hand she's laid on my shoulder and race to the dining room.

"Dan," Tracy pleads. "You can't do this by yourself. You need help. Let me at least call Brian."

"He won't ... He'll just ... " I can't even finish sentences. My mind is racing. How will I find Dustin and Mom? My mom thinks so illogically, she'll be impossible to track.

"Dan, in the parking lot you said she might hurt Dustin. Now they're missing."

"I know!" I turn all my fear and anger, grief and fury on her. "If I hadn't been so busy with your problems, I would have been here to stop her!"

Tracy gasps. Her mouth opening and closing in small spasms. Tears well in her eyes. Her cheeks flush.

I'm immediately sorry. "Tracy, I —"

"I just needed someone to talk to," she says, her voice sullen.

"I know. Me too. I just..." I collapse at the kitchen table and study the papers that line the floor from the hall to the front door. There's no blood or drag marks. No sign of where they went, just drawings, numbers, calculations, and hollow people. I hug Dustin's ratty stuffed dog to my chest, shaking with shock, my burnt hand throbbing under its t-shirt wrapping.

Tracy leans against the wall, crinkling the paper behind her, arms crossed. "You need help."

"But — "

"I'm not going to leave. Now, how do we find them?"

"I wish Mom had left a note," I say. Then I laugh. My mom left nothing but notes. Lots and lots of notes. Not one of them clear or logical or... "Hang on." I run my fingers over the papers on the table. Maybe she was obsessing about where she was going right before she left. Maybe I can find her using the pictures.

On the top paper, pen just to the side, numbers curl like smoke. Fives, threes and sevens, four-teens, twenty-fives, and twenty-sevens drift up in swirls and puffs. She's drawn flames around these numbers. Thick black lines licking and spark-ing upward. Below them is a box. A box on fire. No... not a box. A store. A convenience store. Gupta's Grocery.

Chapter 25

I smell the smoke before I see the fire. Tracy and I race down the sidewalk. Every step feels more and more like a bad dream. The one where no matter how fast I go, I never get closer to where I need to be. We're half a block from Gupta's Grocery when I see the glow. Sparks shoot into the night. An old woman wails.

It's then that I notice the group huddled outside. Chain paces while his mom and sister comfort his grandma, who twists her sari in her fists and cries. I don't see Mr. Gupta, my mom, or Dustin anywhere.

My feet stop. My heart catches. Were they trapped? What if I'm too late? Sirens sound in the distance. Tracy's eyes go wide, like an animal caught in a snare.

"I...I...can't stay," she whispers. "I'm on thin ice with the police already. After the last warning they said... You know..." Her eyes plead for understanding. "I don't want to get blamed for this. I'm sorry, Dan."

I nod. Tracy getting in trouble isn't going to help anything. I watch her fade into a dark side street. And then I'm alone.

I turn back and sprint toward the fire. Chain is the first in his family to spot me. He speeds in my direction, ready to vent his anger.

"You are so dead, Dan!" he screams, thumping me in the side of the head with his fist.

I fall sprawling to the ground. Curl up. Wrap my hands around my head. "Chain, wait!" My voice is muffled between my elbows.

He kicks at my legs. "You were supposed to keep a lid on your schizo mom! Now what am I supposed to do? My home is gone. Our store..." Chain chokes on his words and the worsening smoke. "It was just luck that I was coming home from Padma's when this happened. My family could have died."

"I'm sorry. I'm sorry," I'm screaming. Finally, I realize what Tracy's been saying is true. I can't do this by myself. Would he... "Chain, please... She has my brother." I reach my arm up to him. "Please help me."

He looks at me like I've gone nuts and starts to back away.

"She's going to hurt him. Or worse," I plead.

He shakes his head and grumbles, "Now I'm crazy," before grabbing my arm and yanking me up. "My Dad tried to catch them. I think they went this way. Come on."

Our breath trails white as we race down the street. Fire trucks and police cars pull past us, blaring, making any further conversation impossible. Our faces flicker with orange and red light. We turn down a side street. My lungs throb as night engulfs me. Its darkness eats my hope. *You're not going to make it, you're not going to make it,* is all I can think.

"She's going to jail for this," Chain says, coming to a stop at an intersection and listening, then running on. "You can't protect her."

"I know," I say. "I just want to keep Dustin safe."

"My dad will do that. If he's still with them," Chain replies.

We jog past an alley when I hear a deep East Indian accent. "Why would you harm my family? We have done nothing to you!" Anger flows from the words.

"There!" Chain yells. We back up.

"You nearly killed my wife and my mother! If it hadn't been for my son ... " Mr. Gupta trails off.

His voice is my lifeline. We follow it down the alley until we can see them. Mr. Gupta is talking to Mom from a distance. Mom is backed against a brick wall in just her t-shirt and shorts. Dustin, held tight by her grasp, shivers beside her. He's only wearing his pyjamas and sandals, even though it's near freezing tonight. He looks hypothermic. In Mom's other hand is our biggest kitchen knife, which she is waving close to Dustin's head, its blade marked with numbers. The knife glints off the building's security lights.

"Now, now." I can hear Mr. Gupta struggling to make his voice more soothing, "Put the knife down. You're going to hurt your son. You don't want to do that, now, do you?"

Chain pulls me down behind a truck.

Mom's attention is on Mr. Gupta. She flails the knife in his direction. "I saved you!" she screams, her face twisting. "I warned your mother four days ago. But she wouldn't listen. She wouldn't do what needed to be done. No! Too good for that! So I had to save her, you, the whole universe."

Chain and I creep closer. His idea. "I think we can tackle her by surprise. Just keep low," he whispers.

"But why burn down my store?" Mr. Gupta asks.

Mom huffs. "The evil numbers were pouring into this world and your store was the apex. That was what I was telling your son when you called the police. That was how it spread — through him, into the high school, and into my poor son Daniel."

Dustin turns his head in our direction as we move closer, a relieved grin spreading across his face. "Dan!"

"No, kid," Chain mutters. He melts back. I step forward.

"Mom," I say, "let Dustin go."

"Betrayer!" Mom swings the knife in my direction. "We will escape you!"

"It's me," I plead. "It's Daniel. Your son."

"You may look like my son, but I know who you really are. You are a seven!"

"Come on, you know that's not true." I step closer. Dustin lets out a strangled yelp as Mom yanks at the neck of his pyjama top, tightening it against his throat. I stop.

"Where are your minions?" she demands.

Sirens from two police cars bounce off the alley and pull to a halt behind me. A white sedan appears too. Talk about bad timing.

"Ha!" Mom laughs, moving the knife to slash the air in front of her. "The numbers don't lie!"

My hands are shaking. I'm trying to think of how I can save Dustin without getting stabbed, but my mind is blank and useless. "Mom, stop. Come on."

"I saved the universe," she boasts.

"Yes, you did. We're all safe. You can let Dustin go now."

Her face lights up in rapture. "No, Daniel. I'm taking him to freedom. I am the Sage and he's my apprentice. Together we will become bright fours and sixes."

The police have us surrounded. They bark orders at my mom to drop the knife and let the boy go, but I can tell it's all white noise to her.

"I could be your apprentice too," I say, stepping

toward her, hoping I'll be able to wrench the knife from her grip.

Chain jumps from behind me and rushes my mom, screaming an incoherent war cry. The police tackle him and pull him back.

Mom yells, "Your minions have no power." Then, just for a moment, sadness enters her eyes. She looks like my old mom, back when Dice was around, back when she used to kiss me on the head. "I tried to save you, Daniel," she says.

"I know," I reply, wanting to reach out and hug her.

"But you were going to take Dustin from me." Her eyes narrow and the illness returns.

Dustin wobbles beside her. He looks like he might faint. A woman climbs out of the white car. She's dressed in jeans, a knitted toque, and a puffy parka. She starts begging my mom to do the right thing. To do what's best for Dustin. But what the woman doesn't understand is that Mom thinks she *is* doing what's best. In her mind, she's protecting Dustin.

I'm out of options. Overwhelmed by the noise and light, I start to back up. I shove my hands in my pockets, wincing as my burn slams into something squishy. Pulling it out, I realize it's Dustin's stuffed dog. I must have shoved it in there back at the apartment. Weird — I don't remember doing it.

Mom's screaming and shaking her knife at the woman. The cops have their weapons drawn. I move forward again, holding the dog out in front of me like a shield.

"Dustin," I say.

Mom turns, pointing the knife once more at me.

"Dustin, do you want your dog?"

Dustin lets out a strangled yes.

I look at Mom, questioning. She nods. The police are yelling, maybe at me. Maybe at her. Dustin reaches for his stuffed animal while Mom turns her attention on the cops, moving her knife to threaten them instead. Her fingers loosen on Dustin's top. With a burst of strength and speed, I yank Dustin from her grip, pick him up, and run. One police officer grabs us while his partner shoots a taser. Mom drops. The knife clatters away. More cops handcuff her and drag her to the cruiser.

"Don't hurt her," I beg the officer still holding me. "She's sick."

Dustin begins to slip from my arms. I put him down. The woman from the white car takes his hand and leads him away. Panic replaces my fatigue. "Bring him back!" The woman ignores me, handing Dustin over to the paramedics, who have just arrived.

I rush to the ambulance. "I'm his brother," I tell the paramedic.

"Good." The woman smiles. "You can help with the paperwork."

I spend the next fifteen minutes filling out paperwork, giving statements to the cops, and getting my own wounds checked over.

"You left me," Dustin says, as one of the paramedics moves away to talk with the woman from the white car and the other one tidies up the ambulance.

"I'm sorry." I lift my eyes to the red friction burns on his neck. My gut tightens and guilt fills me. Never again am I going to leave Dustin unprotected. Never.

We sit in silence. Him holding my hand, his dog clutched under his other arm. He gives my fingers a squeeze and I squeeze back. Then he lies back on the stretcher and closes his eyes. "Don't go away," he murmurs before falling asleep.

"Dan, can I talk to you please?" the woman asks.

The woman and I walk a few feet away. The alley is a lot quieter than it was a half-hour ago. The police car with my mom is gone. The cruiser that belongs to the police officers taking statements from Mr. Gupta and Chain remains. I look up at the sky. Most of the smoke has cleared. I can make out a few stars twinkling in the cold night air.

"What do you want?" My anxiety is giving way to exhaustion. I want to go back and shove Dustin over on the stretcher so I can catch some sleep too.

"My name is Violet McCurdy. I work for PAC, an organization that helps kids in crisis."

I look at the ambulance. "We're okay now," I say.

I'll just take Dustin home, call Grandma, and figure out the living arrangements. Crisis averted. Except I get the feeling it's not going to be that easy. Especially since the paramedics just closed the doors and started the engine. I watch them pull away.

Violet looks at me with a kind of hardened sympathy. Like she feels sorry for me but things are going to be by her rules. "Dustin's going to go to the hospital for observation tonight. When he's released tomorrow, I'm taking him into custody," she says.

"But he didn't do anything."

"No, he didn't. But I want to make sure he's safe. You too."

"So, what does that mean? What's safe?" I don't even want to hear what Violet has to say. I feel duped. Like I was lured out of the ambulance so they could take Dustin away. As if he wouldn't be okay with me.

Is this how Mom feels?

Violet's still talking. I realize I missed the beginning. " …and tomorrow we'll have a meeting. He'll either go into foster care or to one of your relatives. Do you have a relative both of you could stay with?"

"My grandma," I say absently.

Violet pulls out her cell phone, ready to dial. "What's her number?"

A shiver runs through me. "I don't know."

Violet frowns.

"We haven't seen her since I was nine! But ... "
I try to calm down. I think of the address book
in my room. "I could go home and get you the
number."

"Okay. When you get it you can reach me
at this number." She hands me a business card.
"Now," she says, "you have a few choices."

"Like what?" Right now I don't feel like I have
any choices.

"Well, you're old enough to decide where you
want to go."

"I want to go with Dustin."

"Not tonight."

"But you just said —"

"You'll get to see him tomorrow for sure. Tonight you need a safe place to be."

Panic hits me square in the chest. They're going to separate us. It's not fair. I want to scream
and rant. I want to find that knife my mom had and
hurt someone. But that's not going to help anyone, I think — least of all Dustin. I wrap my arms
tight around my chest and try to calm down. "I
want to go home."

"Is there anyone at home?"

"No." I shuffle my feet. "So what are my
choices?"

"I can take you to a group home where you can
talk to a counsellor. Or you can go to foster care.
It wouldn't be someone you know, but it would be
safe and you could get some rest. Or, if you have
a friend or relative you're close to, you can stay

with them. Remember, Dan," Violet puts her hand on my shoulder, "it's only for the night. Tomorrow we'll get something more permanent sorted out."

"But Dustin will be scared if I'm not there."

"He's asleep. He probably won't even know you're gone."

Yeah, I've made that mistake before. "Will someone tell him where I am when he wakes up?"

"I'll make sure of it." She holds up her cell phone again. "Now, is there anyone I can call?"

In my head I list all the people that can help me. The list is short. Grandma and Aunt Clara are out for now. Tracy lives in a closet — that's probably not what Violet would consider safe. Even if Chain wanted to help, he's homeless now. I have acquaintances at school, but not many friends. No one I can call, except ... I think back to this afternoon. Heather's mom.

"Call this place," I say, giving her Heather's phone number. "I can probably stay there."

Chapter 26

Karen — Heather's mom — hovers over me, topping up my coffee.

"Mom, seriously," Heather says, shaking her head with embarrassment.

"I'm just making sure Dan's okay," Heather's mom says, putting the coffee pot back on the warmer. "I'll leave you two alone. Make sure you show Dan to the guest room when you're done talking." Karen finally leaves for bed, but not before placing a plate of cookies on the kitchen table.

"So…" Heather says, drawing absently in some spilled cream with her finger. "Psycho mom?"

"Schizo mom. She's schizophrenic," I say, watching her finger. I can't look at her. Can't take the shame of her knowing.

"So did she…" Heather stops and looks up. "Did she do that?" She points to my eye.

"Yeah."

"And that?" She indicates my hand, now expertly bandaged by the paramedics.

I nod.

"Harsh."

"It's not what you think."

Heather looks at me, stunned. "Your mom hurt you and it's not what I think? What is it then?"

"She thought she was helping me."

Heather snorts. "How?"

"You wouldn't get it."

"Not if you don't say anything."

I sigh.

"Dan … I just can't believe … "

"What?"

"You should have told someone. You should have said something. There is no way you and your brother should have lived like that."

My stomach tenses. "And what would you have thought if I had? Huh? You would have run away from me so fast, I would have been eating dust."

"I know now and I'm still here."

"Only because of your mom."

"Only because I care about you, Dan. Seriously, why can't you get that through your head?"

"Aren't you worried I'm crazy too? It's genetic, you know. I might end up just like my mom. I might start spouting numbers any day now. Aren't you freaked about that?" My fists squeeze in my lap. My heart thuds in my ears. "Because I am," I whisper.

"I like you for who you are. Right here. Right now. You protected Dustin. You stood up to your mom. You even got *Chain Gupta* to help you..." Heather lets slip a sly smile. "Actually, maybe you are crazy."

"Yeah, I can't believe I asked him to help. Right after my own mom burned down his store. He's really good in a fight."

Heather shrugs. "It's what he does best."

"I'm sorry, Heather," I say, meeting her eyes. "I should have trusted you."

"Yeah, you should have." She stands and starts for the hall. "I'll show you where the guest room is."

"Actually," I say, "there's somewhere else I need to go first."

***

It's really late when I start the long walk to my apartment. Frost covers everything. Street lights twinkle off the ice crystals in the air, making them look like nocturnal fireflies. I'm going home. No matter what Violet the PAC worker says. There's something I have to do.

When I reach the building, I take the elevator up to the second floor. The hallway is empty and quiet. My skin becomes damp as the ice crystals melt. Standing before my apartment door, I feel sick. I wish this were over.

Violet's business card is still in my pocket.

I could just get the little address book from my room, call Violet with my Grandma's number, and come back out. But that doesn't seem right. This is my life, my family — I should be the one sorting this out. Besides, this mess isn't my fault. I pull out the key, slide it into the lock, and let myself in.

I give a small gasp as toxic marker fumes attack my lungs. The sheer amount of paper still overwhelms me. It's so much — *too* much. One match and this place would burn to the ground. Good thing I'm not a pyromaniac. Good thing Mom wasn't either. An image of Gupta's Grocery flashes through my head, and then I remember what happened.

I start pulling sheets of paper down. Mom won't need these anymore. After all she did, she won't be coming home again. Not for a long, long time. And not here. I can't pay the rent while she's locked up. And even if Grandma won't take me and Dustin in, we're going to have to move.

I spend most of the night tearing paper and tape off the walls, ceiling, windows, doors, cupboards, couch, table, floor. Garbage bag after garbage bag is thrown down the trash chute. Things look almost normal when I finish all the rooms, including Mom's. The salmon pink of an early-morning sky even gives the place a happy glow.

I go into my room and pick up the dirty clothes on the floor, tidy the desk, and take out the pot with mummified spaghetti from last night. Only last night. It feels like so much longer. In the kitchen, I do the dishes one-handed, trying to keep my burn dry. Clean up the spilt noodles, sweep and mop the floor. The house looks great by the time I'm done. It looks like regular people live here. Even the layers of magic marker that bled onto the kitchen table looks like patterned designs rather than signs of illness.

Finally I grab the phone and address book and wedge myself into a corner of the couch. I open the book and find Grandma's number, punch in the digits. I wait while the phone rings again and again. What if there's voice mail? What if it's a wrong number? I move my thumb over the end button, hovering there.

"Hello?" a woman finally answers.

I don't recognize the voice. My heart pounds madly. My breath holds itself in my chest.

"Hello? Who is this?" the woman repeats.

"It's Dan," I finally gasp.

"Dan?" she says. "Dan who?"

"Dan. Daniel. Your grandson."

"Daniel?"

There's confusion in her voice. She doesn't know me. This isn't the right woman. I start to hang up.

"Daniel?" she says again, her voice breaking. "My Daniel?" Then I recognize her by the way she says my name. I hear her hiccup as she tries to hold back a sob. "Daniel. Where is your mother?"

Chapter 27

No Internet, no TV, no video games, and two horrible cousins. It's taken a day and a half for me to lose my mind.

"Daniel, stop playing that bass guitar and get out here!" Aunt Clara calls. I know she and Grandma have been talking about me. And I already know what my vote is — I've got to get out of this place.

I wander into the large, brightly-lit living room and collapse on the chair across from Grandma, Aunt Clara, and Uncle Larry. They sit like they're some kind of jury and I'm the one on trial. Outside the window I spot a deer, making tracks in the fresh backyard snow. It's very scenic, but I'm desperate for civilization.

"Daniel..." my aunt begins.

"It's Dan," I correct.

"Whatever." She waves her hand in front of her

face before running her fingers through her short, dark hair. "Your grandma, Uncle Larry, and I have been talking about what's best for you and your brother."

Grandma takes a sip of her coffee. She looks a lot like my mom, except with white hair, a few more wrinkles, and eyes that actually look at you steadily. Uncle Larry looks like a politician. Straight-cut hair and a suit, even though it's the weekend and church is over.

"The nearest high school," Aunt Clara continues, "is an hour away by school bus and I'm worried you might not get your studying done with all the little kids around."

"We thought you might want to live with me," Grandma says. "It's a small house, but walking distance to a high school and on a bus route, so you can still see your friends."

"But what about Dus—"

Running feet and screaming drown out my words. Charlie and Thompson, my seven- and nine-year-old cousins come tearing into the living room. Thompson has my bass guitar slung over his shoulder, the cord from the amp trailing behind him. He jumps, legs apart, and throws down a muted power chord. "I'm a rock star!" he declares.

Rage begins to rise in my chest. I leap up to throttle him when Dustin comes skittering into the room, socks sliding on the hardwood floor. "I told you," he yells at Thompson, "leave my brother's bass alone!"

Dustin jumps on Thompson and Charlie throws himself into the mix. It's all I can do to rescue my poor bass before it's snapped in two.

"Hey," Thompson says, pulling himself from the tangle. "Wanna play road hockey?"

"Yeah!" Charlie and Dustin cheer, and, fight forgotten, they all charge out of the room.

"Put on your snow pants, it's cold out there!" Aunt Clara yells after them.

Grandma smiles. "Those boys are a blessing." She turns to me. "So what do you think, Dan?"

"Um…" I say, looking at Thompson's name crayoned onto my bass. "I think living with you might be a good idea."

Heading back to the bedroom to pack what little I have, I dodge Dustin hopping around as he pulls on his snow pants.

"Do you like it here?" I ask, leaning my bass up against the wall.

He beams at me, his smile so wide it makes him look like a totally different kid. "This is the best place ever!"

"I'm not staying," I say. My chest tightens up. I'm afraid of his reaction. His smile barely slips.

"I kind of figured. Thompson keeps getting into your stuff."

"You don't mind?" I ask.

Dustin shakes his head. "Why should I? You don't have to look after me anymore."

"Yeah," I say. "I guess not."

"Now we can be normal brothers," Dustin says,

"like Charlie and Thompson."

"Them, normal?" I ask. "Normal like this?" I grab him and throw him on the bed, giving him a noogie on the head with my knuckles. Dustin squeals, giggling madly, before squirming away and running out of the room, returning only briefly to stick his tongue out at me and yell, "Come and play hockey with us when you're done!"

Epilogue

Gupta's Grocery, now new and bright, stands before me. Behind me, Maggie revs her truck. She's anxious to get going — we're running late, but I made her stop. This is the first time I've seen the new store. The first time I've been here since the fire. Chain sells a kid a pack of gum, then looks up through the plate-glass windows and spots me. He ducks out from behind the counter, exiting into the warm evening air of early summer. I back up a step.

"Dan," he says.

"Chain. Nice place. So the insurance covered everything?"

He shakes his head. "Nah, but my cousins from India chipped in too."

I peer past him. "Hey, you have a working slush machine."

"First time in three years. I'm glad I don't

have to keep changing the 'Out of Order' sign anymore." Chain raises an eyebrow, "So, is your mom still ... ?"

"Yeah. I haven't seen her for a while. Look, I'm sorry about what my m—"

Chain puts up his hand. "Don't worry about it. At least she's getting help. I just don't know how you lived with that. If it had been me, I'd have been pissed."

"Yeah, sometimes it felt like she liked her numbers more than me."

"Harsh."

"Then I feel guilty for thinking that."

Chain leans in, his voice hushed, "I know what you're talking about. When my grandma has her 'bad omen' days, I just want to tell her to snap out of it. But then I think: maybe I should be more understanding."

"Chain!" a voice calls from down the street.

I look up and see Chain's gang, with Padma leading the way.

"You should go," Chain says.

"Yeah, see ya. And ... thanks for the help."

"No problem," Chain smiles. "Good luck tonight. It sounds like fun. Maybe I'll even come."

"Huh?" I ask, confused, until I see the poster for our band's gig taped in the window beside a sign for pet care. Heather said she had spread posters all around this area, I just didn't think Chain would have put one up. Climbing back into Maggie's truck, I wonder what it would be like if he came — Chain stage-diving into a mosh pit. It makes me laugh.

"Ready to go *now*?" Maggie asks, pulling away.

"Yeah." I nod. "Let's do this thing."

At the Night Owl, Heather sips coffee at the side of the stage, hands trembling. She's been nervous about our first gig all week. I finish setting up my bass and head over to her, sliding my fingers across a worn Vancouver postcard pinned to the nearby wall. Tracy flickers through my mind. It's been months since that postcard arrived.

Gordon, the owner of the Night Owl, comes by, wafting his Playboy cologne through the air. "You and your band ready, Dan?"

Maggie is already sitting at her drums. Sebastian, head to head with Farmer discussing power chords, gives me a nod and moves to the front of the stage. I wrap my arm around Heather. "Ready?"

"Sure," she smiles.

"Good," Gordon says, gesturing at the stage. "Anytime."

My hands are sweaty and my adrenalin is surging, but this time, it feels good. Heather gives me a weak smile and I grin back. The place is crowded. Farmer whoops and whistles. Heather takes a deep breath, swings her long hair around her head, and my girlfriend is transformed into a metal queen. With a demonic lilt, she introduces the band, and we break into "Psycho Mom."

The crowd cheers and the mosh pit begins to swirl. Maggie pounds out time and Sebastian lets his guitar scream. My fingers fly over the frets, laying down the bass line. When Heather starts singing, pure happiness fills me. Life couldn't get any better. I'm grinning like a real idiot — and then I see Chain Gupta rush into the café, push his way through the crowd, and start to climb onto the stage.

Read more great teen fiction from SideStreets.

Ask for them at your local library or bookstore, or order them online at www.lorimer.ca.

Final Takedown
by Brent R. Sherrard

The judge has given Elias a warning: Shape up, or do time in juvie. But how's a guy to keep out of trouble when his mom's an alchie, he's kicked out of school, and his best friend wants him to join in on a takedown that he knows isn't going to work?
ISBN: 978-1-55277-523-3 (paperback)

Scab
by Robert Rayner

Julian Faye, aka Scab, knows all about being picked on. For years he's been bullied by his classmates and neglected by his parents. Now seventeen and a gifted photographer, he's faced with a dilemma: Get the shot that'll launch his career, or save the only person who's ever cared about him.
ISBN: 978-1-55277-482-3

Ceiling Stars
by Sandra Diersch

Christine and Danelle have been friends forever. Danelle's always been the wacky one, pushing 'Prissy Chrissy' to loosen up, to have some real fun. But now Christine's scared — Danelle's ideas go way beyond fun. How far will Christine go to make her best friend happy?
ISBN: 978-1-55028-834-6 (paperback)

 LORIMER